CHEERLEADERS
FROM GOMORRAH

CHEERLEADERS FROM GOMORRAH

Tales from the Lycra Archipelago

JOHN REMBER

A James R. Hepworth Book

CONFLUENCE PRESS

ACKNOWLEDGMENTS

Previous incarnations of all stories herein, except for "Shadowman" and "M.I.A.," were published in the *Idaho Mountain Express*. "Banshee" appeared in *Redneck Review*. "Idaho Man" appeared in *Boise Magazine*.

Publication of this book is made possible by grants from Lewis-Clark State College; the Idaho Commission on the Arts, a State agency; and the National Endowment for the Arts in Washington, D.C., a Federal agency.

ISBN: 1-881090-03-5 (cloth)
ISBN: 1-881090-06-x (paper)

Library of Congress Card Number 93-71409

Cover art Copyright © 1994 by Lisa Lawerance

Cover design by Karla Fromm
Interior design and production by Tanya Gonzales

Published by:

Confluence Press, Inc.
Lewis-Clark State College
500 8th Avenue
Lewiston, Idaho 83501-2698

Distributed to the trade by:

National Book Network
4720-A Boston Way
Lanham, Maryland 20706

Except the Lord of hosts had left unto us a very small remnant, we should have been as Sodom, and we should have been like unto Gomorrah.

Isaiah 1:9

CONTENTS

CHEERLEADERS
FROM GOMORRAH

PUNKIN LOOKS TO THE FULL-LENGTH mirror and sees long feathers of blonde hair. And white and even teeth. And blue eyes. And lips that have relaxed to an adenoidal pout, and cheek-size starbursts of freckles. And all of these on a gold-colored body that weighs a hundred pounds and is five feet tall. She sees sturdy little pink-tipped breasts, a round little ass and strong stocky little legs.

She dances forward, tosses her hair, and smiles a question at the mirror. The mirror smiles back. "You're cute," it says. "Completely cute. Terminally cute." Snow White should have been so lucky.

Punkin makes a quick whirl to the sliding glass door behind her, opens it, and steps out on the balcony of her condo. A fat sun is about to disappear over the mountains and leave all of town in warm shadow. Cottonwood fluff lies in tiny dunes on the balcony railing. Smells of barbecue from neighbors' balconies, of exhaust from cars and motorhomes, of the newly-cut grass at the park, and Punkin's perfume—a Chanel knockoff that to men smells like the real thing—have all blended in the air. Punkin loves summer.

Halfway across the quarter-mile of grass that stretches from her condo to the cottonwood fringe of the river, boys are kicking a soccer ball. Like dogs on a fox, thinks Punkin. She suddenly sees, brilliant there in the distance, a savage game, where small animals with sharp teeth have been set loose in a flag-draped arena. They're being kicked about by naked young men, watched from high above by princesses.

One of the boys sees her, shouts to another, and points right at her. Punkin turns and slowly walks back inside. Some nights, home alone from the bars, she's undressed and swept her drapes open, and searched the darkness behind the sliding glass door for an honest man. Nothing. What do you do with a creep who's struggled up to your balcony, once he's frozen there by your eyes? You touch the glass softly, sliding your nails across the spot where his face presses against it.

She goes to her phone and dials her friend Angel's number. It rings four times. Angel's a weaver, and—Punkin's joke—gets tied up in her work. Angel finally answers, the sleep of weaving in her voice: "Uh-huh?"

"It's time," says Punkin.

"Time?" asks Angel. "Time for what?" Lots of people don't think Angel's at all bright, but she is. Punkin's had to explain that to men, when Angel's decided she didn't like them.

"Time to hunt unicorns," says Punkin.

"I'll be by," says Angel, and hangs up. Punkin looks at the phone, wishing she'd told Angel to just meet her on Main Street. Punkin has waited hours, sometimes, while Angel's picked out just what to wear.

But the night is young. Punkin goes to her own closet, pulls on a pair of hiking shorts, then goes back to the mirror. In other places—the best ones, she thinks—women go bare-breasted.

Finally she sorts through her pile of clean laundry and grabs a T-shirt a river guide has given her. It's got a boat and rapids silkscreened on it. Punkin's been on whitewater expeditions and has been taught how to row a float boat. One of these years she's going to get her guide's license. In the meantime, all the real guides know who she is, and she gets a river trip every time one of them makes a run at her.

"So why don't you take a real lover?" Angel has asked, when Punkin has complained about sleeping all alone.

Punkin's got a stuffed unicorn on her dresser, all white, with aquamarine eyes. In dreams, he comes to life, whispers to her, walks with her in fields of golden flowers, carries her—her fingers entwined in his mane—across tumbling rivers, sleeps with his hooves folded under his chest and his head outstretched across her lap. "Remember my name," he tells her, "and I'll come to you when you call." But he never tells her his name, or if he does she can't remember it. She *would* take a real lover, she tells Angel, except the ones with white hair and blue eyes are always too old.

Punkin would sleep with her unicorn, but she thinks he might get tumbled about, and begin losing all his hair, and like the Velveteen Rabbit, start looking scroungy and too much-loved. Once Angel took Punkin's unicorn from the dresser, hugged him, held him high above her on outstretched arms while lying back on Punkin's bed, until she sensed, in Punkin's gaze, a thing violated, and, without having to be told, never touched the unicorn again.

Punkin's passed men on to Angel. She's met them in bars and they've looked at her and asked the central question: How Single Are You? And she's given the central answer: As Single As You Can Get. They've always taken it wrong. Sometimes, sparked to gentleness, she has taken them over and introduced them to Angel, and they've never come back to bother her. And Angel isn't even cute.

Angel is, however, twenty-four, tall and Indian-looking, long-limbed and big-assed, with big sloping breasts that gravity won't forgive and soft eyes, too, and a soft voice. Men consider her a beautiful aborigine, and don't believe her when she says she's Jewish and from Babylon. They fall in love with her and ask her to marry them. She says maybe, encourages them with presents of hats or moccasins she's made for them, keeps them happy with her big breasts and big ass, until one day, she takes off with someone else who's in love with her, someone she's met in a bar, someone, maybe, introduced to her by Punkin.

Punkin envies Angel, not for the men Angel has in love with her, but for Angel's ability to walk away from any one of them untouched and complete. Punkin's had men fall in love with her too, but she's never been able to leave one of them without feeling for him the tearing pain of his grief. And that isn't the worst of it—Punkin's left men because she couldn't stand them touching her, couldn't stand them up close. A river guide or ski patrolman who looked so good across the room, all tanned skin and muscles and thick hair and good teeth, would turn into pore-ridden flesh and beer breath at the distance of a kiss.

And Punkin's thirty. Men her age are getting too old for her. She takes grey hair on a man as an insult. When they're bald or wrinkled or grey, and more and more of them are these days, and they call to her and wrap their arms around her—then she pulls away from herself and watches over her own shoulder, watches a maiden be embraced by Old Man Death Himself. Punkin goes to the bars to look for young ones, the ones who, in hope or ignorance, think she's nineteen. And with those, she pulls back to watch herself in the arms of Fools.

Punkin's excited by the idea that people can be dipped in liquid nitrogen and set to thaw sometime in the future, when people live forever and everybody has personal wings. These days, of course, it's messy. That man—some accountant, Punkin thinks—who had his mother's head cut off and frozen before she was dead—Punkin wants a technology a little more advanced than that, something on the order of a time-closet you can walk into in early fall, stand still for a few heartbeats, and walk out into the heavy smells of late spring. A lifetime of summers. She'd give up skiing to have it.

Punkin skips across her living room and looks out the window to see if Angel's car is in the parking lot. It isn't. There is always the danger that Angel has gone back to her weaving, where, she has explained to Punkin, time goes differently.

Lots of things go differently for Angel. "This is what we're doing," Angel has told Punkin, making weaving motions in the air. And Punkin hasn't understood. "This world," Angel has said, "we're weaving it." And then Punkin has peered into the air between Angel's hands and has seen the silk and the shimmer of strands.

Punkin thinks maybe she's using too coarse a material for the men she's been weaving to life, the ski patrolmen and fly-fishing guides and hang-glider pilots and triathletes. Town is full of them. It's not fair that she might be responsible for the existence of them all. Maybe, thinks Punkin easily, happily, it's the other way around. They're responsible for me.

Once, Angel took Punkin home to Babylon with her. Punkin ended up talking in some dirty little storefront coffee shop to some friend of Angel's, some fat guy, some black guy, some artist, who had bad teeth and pimples and a frown on his face when he looked at her. She'd just finished telling him that at home she was a ski instructor and river guide and free climber and mountain bike racer—when he looked across the table and said: "Shit. You just know people who do those things." Punkin didn't tell him he was right. She just looked at Angel and said it was time to go.

Punkin's watched Angel weave, and thinks Angel isn't really working at the loom, isn't actually weaving anything, but has instead gone inside herself and is hanging out in a theme park there. She's got free tickets to all the rides, up the Matterhorn, through the jungle, into the starship. What takes shape on the loom is nothing but snapshots and souvenirs. She's sure that one day Angel will get lost inside, get stuck on herself in the Tunnel of Love or something, and when she finally finds a way out she will have stayed too long in a place where time works differently, and will come out to a huge red sun and to men who are small, bent, hairy, and crazed.

Nothing could be worse.

Punkin, impatient, goes to the phone and dials Angel's number again. The second ring triggers Angel's answering machine.

"What was your name before your mother and father were born?" asks Angel's voice. "Tell me what it is, and I'll get back to you."

Angel must have found something to wear. Punkin goes to a closet and pulls out a pair of lightweight hiking boots and puts them on. They're for dancing. When she's worn sandals or moccasins, she's gotten her toes stepped on. Hiking boots go well with what she's wearing anyway. Punkin thinks if she lived in Babylon, she could get a job as a model for the REI catalog. She should send them a picture.

There are nights Punkin sees herself as a a spark on a dark dance floor, bouncing in front of the band, never going out, giving heat and light and good feelings to men as she moves close to them. She begins a dance with one and ends with another, her hair shaken over her face, blind to who she's dancing with, untouched inside a blonde wall she grew herself. Sometimes she just walks out alone and dances right in front of the lead singer, dances with the band, dances close, dances just inside the spotlights, so that it's just the band and Punkin, just Punkin and the band, bright among all the others in the darkness, and that's all that seems to happen while a song goes on.

So unicorns are really hard to find. Sometimes there are only signs, hints, smudged names on deeds or property tax rolls. Angel says there are houses in town with white rugs on the glassy, fire-reflecting floors of their living rooms, and on their walls are the severed heads of rhinos and simple frames holding small Picassos. In their garages Range Rovers and Ferraris. Their owners are hidden in third-floor stalls, secluded behind the black glass of limousines, flown into and out of town in specially-equipped Lear jets, which Punkin herself has seen at the airport.

However, Angel says you can see the signs of whole worlds, sometimes, in the strands that collect under your fingernails. So nothing is sure. So you should never dare to plan for success on a unicorn hunt. Punkin hears the slamming of a car door in the parking lot and the soft pad of feet on the stairs. A shadow appears at her door, opens it, and walks in.

Angel's wearing feathers and crystals. She's got chains on her wrists, flowers at her neck, small points of metal in her hair. She's got beaded moccasins on her feet and is wearing iridescent white running tights, and a long belted pullover she's woven out of white cotton rope. It looks like chain mail. Angel's a knight, covered with favors and charms against dragons. Punkin giggles. All of Main Street is lined with lairs.

Dragons will be out tonight, checking I.D.s, collecting cover, bartending. For a kiss they'll let you in the door. For a pat on the ass they'll comp you drinks all night long. Pass out at a table and they'll volunteer to see you safely home. Dragons go hunting when hunters hunt unicorns.

Angel walks to Punkin, puts her hands on Punkin's shoulders, bends down and kisses the top of Punkin's head. Punkin, being kissed, touches Angel's arms with her fingertips and wonders how it is that the texture of a woman is so different from the texture of a man. She wonders if tonight, in that part of town Angel calls Frustrated Desire, she'll avoid the dragons long enough to meet a unicorn smooth to her touch, whose presence won't tear her into fragments, who will let her live in her own body. She wonders if he'll hold her close and whisper in her ear the magic sounds of his name. And finally, looking up into the bright and shining eyes of Angel, Punkin wonders: Is she weaving me now?

As if in answer, Angel grasps Punkin's hands and leads her out the door. Glowing sharp against the sudden darkness, moving across the video screen of night, Punkin becomes a thread, a long bright strand, drawn down and back and forth across the fixed warp of the world.

ZOMBIE

HARDESTY'S GOT HIS HEART BROKE. That's a name for it, anyway. Suzanne—the beautiful Suzanne he's been calling his own—has just threatened to burn down his house, sugar the gas tank of his car, and tell every other woman in town that funny little birthmark on his rear is Kaposi's Sarcoma. All because she thinks she's wasted her late twenties with him. She wants something to show for those years, wants a child, marriage, wants him to get a real job because she's tired of him being on unemployment half the year, wants him to do something with his life besides wander through the backcountry on skis, does he understand, DO SOMETHING, like fix the window on the back porch that's been letting the cold in for two winter months now....

And so, an hour later, Hardesty's out for a solo moonlight ski. He's high up the valley above the neon glitter of Gomorrah, Idaho, traversing his way up a bowl on the side of a peak called Lot's Wife. A full moon is shining between patches of drifting fog. A storm has dropped two feet of heavy snow, and then cleared, leaving him a bright world marked only by the dark forms of perpendicular rocks and trees. His skis sink deep with each step, and he hears the snow constantly settling, collapsing into itself, sometimes for yards around him.

He has a sudden grim thought. It's below zero already, and he's out alone, and the bars closed an hour ago and everybody he knows is with new friends in a warm bed or hot tub. It's Singles Week in Gomorrah.

It'll be Suzanne's fault if he falls into a tree well and, and unable to move, freezes to death. And then there's the new snow to think about. Its surface drops with a whump! ahead of him, and fracture lines snap out like black lightning from his ski tips. I'll probably die, thinks Hardesty. It'll be just what she deserves.

Hardesty gets warm just thinking about the injustice of it all. It's his house she's nagging him to fix, his signature on the marriage license she wants, his job she wants him working fifty weeks a year, his life, he thinks, that she wants to find her identity in. He thinks of all of his sad little sperm cells who have run into latex dams that didn't have fish ladders, or who have been crushed by her IUD, or who believed the lethal lies of her Pills—now she's giving them names, dressing them up in doll clothes and hearing their tiny voices call her Mommy. Why, he thinks, do women have to get old?

Hardesty tries to articulate what he feels.

"AAARRRAAAGGAAA!" he screams, and he hears the sound echoed from across the bowl he's in, from the high cliffs above him, and then, diminished to a long sigh, from far above the cliffs.

I love that woman, Hardesty thinks, remembering a time when love was easily relieved. Then he hears a sound like low-level feedback over a rock concert sound system. He looks up and sees hundred-foot plumes of boiling snow and snapping trees. Ten acres of snow, piled into a tumbling mass, cascade over the steep frozen rock of Lot's Wife, right at him.

He looks around, sees fifty feet away the dark trunk of a giant Doug fir, trimmed of limbs thirty feet up by last year's avalanche. He starts toward it, not panicking because he knows—yup, he's gonna die. No sense worrying about that, just take nice long strides, that's right, halfway there now, speed it up a little, keep the skis straight, that's right. Not that it's going to do any good.

He manages three or four more drift-slowed steps before the big wind hits him, and a half step more before it knocks him down. His mouth and nose are blown full of snow. There's a screaming around him, broken by the loud splintering popping of frozen wood. The Doug Fir is whisked out of his sight, and he feels his feet being twisted by his skis—something's trying to tear them off.

And then he's under. Snow is pushing down his neck and big chunks of—ice or rock, maybe—are hitting him in the ribs and kidneys. He feels himself somersaulting over and over, but it's in slow motion, and the snow is trying to roll him into a ball. His arms and legs are moving but he's not moving them. There's still noise—a roaring—but it's getting fainter and fainter. He tries to put his hands over his face but he no longer knows where his hands are or where his head is. His skis are twisting away, and he hopes the bindings go before the bones—.

And then everything is quiet except a loud whispering of snow sliding against snow. He's still moving, fast, he thinks, floating down soft rapids in some great river of frozen air. He catches a glimpse of bright silver light and he remembers stories he's been told about people dying and then finding, at the end of a tunnel, the most wonderful and warmest imaginable divine being and getting to meet long dead pets and family members, but then hearing a still-living child's cry or remembering a casserole left smoking on the stove and having to go back. But he, Hardesty, is not going back. This is it, he thinks. My head has already been removed back a few hundred yards. He rides along, turning and tumbling, thinking to himself how painless his death has been so far and how lucky he is that it happened to happen the way it's happening.

But then he stops. Real sound comes back to his world, but it's only the high whimpering scream he starts making when he realizes his head is still on and his eyes are open and he can't see anything but black. His face and neck and head come alive to the deep and nauseating shock of too much snow. He's buried. He doesn't know how deep. One leg is bent under him—it's okay, it's bent in the right direction—but he can't move it. Body cast, he thinks. Of ice.

It's over, thinks Hardesty. I really am dead. Except I'm not done dying yet. And it's not going to be painless at all.

With difficulty, he pulls cold air into his nose through packed snow. He knows that when he exhales, the snow will melt and freeze and then melt and freeze again until in a few minutes his face will be covered by an ice mask and he will stop being able to breathe at all. Then a great straining, a series of silent and still convulsions, and the end of all his thoughts.

Suzanne. He sees her at his funeral—sometime in April or May, if they find him before the coyotes do. She's crying, tossing a shovelful of dirt onto his coffin with a lightweight backcountry snow shovel. Lots of his telemark buddies there too, saying things like HE SHOULDA DUG A SNOW PIT, or HE SHOULDNA GONE UP WHEN THE CONDITIONS WERE LIKE THAT, MAN THAT'S JUST ASKING FOR TROUBLE.

Hardesty realizes he's going to belong to them now, to the Nordic Patrol as an all-purpose bad example, brought up at meetings to prove what everybody knows, that a person can die out there at night and alone, especially when he gets hit by a climax slide coming off the spine of Lot's Wife. And to Suzanne, who will make a little shrine for him on his mantle, with framed telemark scenes, and maybe have his ski boots bronzed. She'll say they wanted to have a baby, say they were going to get married, say he promised her she could live in his house forever. Hardesty can't stand it.

He tries to breathe through his mouth and sucks snow dust into his lungs. Starts coughing, gagging. Lifts his head. Takes a deep breath. And another.

What's this? Another light? Moonlight? Hardesty dares to open his eyes again and it—sure enough—really is moonlight, coming in streamers through a haze of tiny frost particles still hanging in the air. He's ridden the avalanche down the side of the peak, with only helpless good luck keeping him afloat on its shifting back. Without even knowing it, he's just body surfed a wave a hundred times bigger than any at Waikiki. He's face down, half buried, drifted over by six inches of sugary snow, cold and shaking but alert.

With a huge effort, he pushes himself to his knees, and the snow that had molded to his back and hips falls away. His legs won't move. They're still buried. Something is holding them deep under the snow and he's overcome by a thick terror that he's trapped, stuck, able to breathe only long enough for him to freeze to death. Then, with a sudden joy, he realizes that it's his skis that are holding him, that they haven't been torn off by the avalanche, and he might get off The Wife alive after all. He digs packed snow away from them and finally shakes a ski back and forth until it comes free. When he finally frees the other ski, he discovers that its tip is bent back on itself. It's going to make it hard to make a decent set of tracks down out of here.

His poles are gone. He looks around for a bit of bright plastic against the snow, but there's nothing. He looks down the jumble of the avalanche, as far as he can see, and still nothing. He kicks harder and feels something hard. Ski pole, he thinks. He lunges at it and grabs wood. It's only a broken branch. He has, he thinks, spent his all his luck for this evening.

His lungs hurt and his shoulders and knees are stiffening. No fractures, though, at least none he can feel. He's very cold. He checks his hands, maybe for the second time, and only now realizes his gloves are gone, pulled off by the ski pole straps that were around them. The hands they covered are numb.

He stands up on his skis and brushes as much snow as he can out of his turtleneck and the hood of his parka. The cloth, wet with sweat and skin-melted snow, is starting to freeze.

With hands that now won't work unless they're watched, he reaches down and strips off his climbing skins, wads them up and thrusts them, in a stuck-together jumble, into his pocket. He steps forward, starts to slide and falls. Balance still isn't there. He sits in the snow, hands in his armpits, and begins to shake.

Forget the poles. Forget the gloves. They're nowhere to be seen. They could be right under his feet and he could die searching for them. He's beginning to have little fits of uncontrollable shivering.

He stands up, slides his skis back and forth a few times to make sure everything works, sticks both hands in his parka pockets, and eases down the broken surface of the slide in an unsteady traverse. There's smooth powder on the side of the bowl. When he reaches it he begins a quick descent, balancing back on the bent ski so it doesn't arrow into the snow, turning only when he has to slow down because he can't see what is below.

At the top of a big knoll he stops. He looks down at two hundred yards of steep powder broken only by small scattered trees. At the bottom he can see black lines—his tracks—at the end of the logging road he came up on. He heads his skis straight for it.

By the time he skis onto the road, his skis are singing with speed against the frosted crystals on the surface of the snow. And when he hits the road's flat surface, his bent ski punches forward and down, and he pitches forward, over his ski tips, somersaulting, flipping back to his feet, pitching forward again and sticking head-first in the snow. For a moment he's in the avalanche once more, struggling to breathe. Then, cursing, he extricates his hands from his pockets, untangles his skis, and pushes himself to his knees. He thinks of the long moment when he thought he had died and traveling was easier. He sees the avalanche carrying him down, down, further down, through the alleys and streets of Gomorrah, over the restaurants and storefronts, safe to his home.

Then he's shivering again, clasping and unclasping his fingers, trying to feel something from them. He gets to his feet, suddenly worried that after all this luck and effort, he still won't make it. He thinks his brain is starting to cool toward the temperature of dreams—he could have sat there and remembered the avalanche and remembered its soft and gentle side forever.

He has to keep moving, he tells himself. Too much energy gone. Last week, hungry on the way home from climbing the peak known as Eve's Serpent, he ate the emergency chocolate in his pack.

He steps into the slots of his tracks and heads for his car. Just a mile to go and it's steep enough that it's all fast. Tears stream out of his eyes and freeze on his cheeks. Here and there trees shadow the road and he slides muttering with fear into black corners, terrified that he's going to end up straddling something big.

By the time he gets to the roadside turnout where he's parked his car, he's shaking and he can't stop shaking, shaking so violently it's hard to stand on his skis and he knows that soon the shaking will suddenly stop and he'll feel calm and so good that he'll forget the car, forget where he is, and follow another bright light.

He hits the steep slope of plowed snowbank on the road edge. His skis slip backwards and he falls, hands still in pockets, his shoulder jamming onto his ski tip. With his elbow he pushes himself back on his knees, rocks to his feet, and stands staring at a nervous, shuddering moon until finally he remembers where he is and sidesteps up over the snowbank and drops down to the ice of the road.

He pops off his skis and fumbles at the zipper of the pocket his keys are in. Maybe the keys won't be there, he thinks. Maybe they're gone, lost forever under ice and the broken limbs of shattered fir, and they will find me here, huddled over the hood of my car, trying to get the last bit of heat from a dead engine. But the keys are in his pocket. He pulls them out, and thinks, maybe the door won't open. Maybe the keyhole is full of ice. But the key slides in and the door swings open, and when he falls into the driver's seat he realizes the inside of the car is warmer than the outside air and then he realizes that on some deep level, he believed he'd never feel any kind of warmth again. He watches his hand, looking and feeling as if it belongs to someone else, grab the steering wheel and pull him onto the seat. And the car starts and—hey, what a relief—there's gas enough to get to town.

In another five minutes he's got his skis on the roof rack. Warm air is coming out of the heater ducts. Big quaking shudders are going through his body and a welcome pain is oscillating up his arms from his warming hands. I'm alive, he thinks.

He says it aloud: "I'm alive."

Hardesty grins in the darkness, pulls the car out onto the road, and heads for town at twenty-five miles an hour.

He should be among the dead. He's been to their still, snow-drifted land, has felt their sudden mindless clutch, has been caught in their cold furious violence, has known his life was done. And now every new minute is one he's free to float through as he wishes, a bonus point, a piece of time bought and paid for with his death.

Things he's not going to do: Marry Suzanne, give her a baby, get a real job, or fix that fucking window. Then he remembers he wasn't going to do any of them anyway.

It's the last few months of life with Suzanne. She's been reading whole chapters of her co-dependency books to him, coming home from her Women Who Love Too Much meetings and staring right through him, asking him if he thinks he's going to be young forever, telling him he can't spend every day skiing, can he? Some people have real lives, she tells him.

When he's tried to take her out telemarking, she's ended up screaming at him from the top of steep chutes, saying he's trying to get her lost, trying to leave her in a place where she'd be all alone, trying to kill her—it's been days before she's calmed down—when he was just wanting to show her how beautiful it was out there, and how quiet. Secure men, she's been telling him, ride ski lifts.

He remembers a season pass on Gomorrah's ski hill, Mount Mammon, used until one last late March trip down to the afterski party at the base lodge in Moloch Gulch, first quickly down the big moguls of Hellfire, then onto the sharp bumps on the high south side of Mephistopheles, jumping the cat tracks, diving screaming back through the crowd on the track to the top of Ishtar, fast enough to get lots of air, a realization: THIS IS BORING.

So what isn't? Lately he's been ski jumping off backcountry cliffs for kicks, tumbling eighty or a hundred feet before sticking into the snow, hoping no rocks or tree stumps are near the surface. He's been dancing on the cornices above the Lethe Creek Burn, trying to get something started. It makes people nervous. Lately he's begun to have to go out alone.

So tonight he can remember telling Suzanne, "Wait a minute. Stop," because he doesn't care what it is that's upset her anymore. And then he can remember walking away and into the bathroom and staring for a long moment in the mirror above the sink, wondering what he could possibly look like to her. A husband? Father? Fixer-of-windows? A terror has been growing in him that she's been with him all this time and she doesn't have the slightest idea of who he is or what he thinks. He stares into the mirror and knows, with a sudden despair, that he cannot answer those questions either.

But he's been resisting being cast in her dreams for a long time, joking with himself about being the Passive Aggression Poster Boy, telling himself she'll start liking him as soon as she gives up on him filling any voids in her own life—he quotes things back to her

that she's read to him, psychotheraputic homilies about uncon-
ditional love or conscious betrayal, and it makes her mad as hell.
He smiles.

But no. There's nothing fun about it anymore. Because tonight
he remembers coming out of the bathroom quickly and stopping
her before she could say anything else.

"Get out," he remembers saying. "Please get out of my house.
Get your stuff and go. Please."

He remembers thinking that if he were polite, it was going to
be that simple. But half an hour later she was yelling, through
tears and out of a face that had turned some caring part of him to
cold stone, "Six wasted years. Six wasted years of my life.

And finally he put on his ski clothes, laced his boots, fastened
his gaiters, and looked out the window for the big moon. She
walked beside his car as he backed out of the driveway, saying
things low and deadly, but he had rolled up the window and he
thought, a little surprised because he could see her and the ugly
twist of muscle behind her once-smooth face so clearly: I can't
hear her anymore.

So now he's almost warm. He can feel something other than
pain from his hands. The heater's working well. There's a buzzing
coming from the engine compartment, and he realizes—
whoops—he drove all the way into town in low gear. Funny what
getting cold will do to your brain.

He finds himself among the lights of town. Tea, he thinks. Tea
for hypothermia. Recommended by four out of five members of
the Nordic Patrol. I'll make some as soon as I'm home. I'll fix
myself some tea and sit. I'll put lots of sugar in it. I'll get well.
Suzanne will be have cried herself to sleep and I won't wake her, and
I'll sleep on the couch and maybe I, back from the dead, will look
different to her in the morning.

But when Hardesty gets to his house the lights are all out and
the doors and windows are all open. Suzanne has turned off the
furnace and poured water in the woodstove. She's stuffed rags in
the sink and left the faucets running. When he steps in the front
room he steps into a freezing lake, one that's dribbling downstairs

into his basement bedroom. His TV, its picture tube smashed, sits on the kitchen floor with a rim of ice around it.

He runs into the kitchen and turns off the water. Shuts all the doors and windows. Starts the furnace and fires up the woodstove with a couple of wax-and-sawdust condo logs. Turns on lots of lights. Down in the basement a sump pump is running—he can hear it, and tries to remember being the kind of person he must have been when agreed with Suzanne that he should install it.

He looks around. It's going to be all right. Suzanne has insisted he keep his insurance up, and now he knows why. He goes into the kitchen and makes himself a cup of tea, with a lot of sugar.

Hardesty's got his boots off and has his feet propped up on the kitchen table—there's an inch of water on the floor and the biggest terror in his life right now is that he's going to get his socks wet. A quart of hot tea gurgles in his stomach. The woodstove glows redly on its hearth behind him. He grins.

He remembers what has happened to him, thinks again of the great white cloud as it came over the rocks above him, sees himself in out-of-body slow motion as he hurries toward the tree, watches the chaos of ice and dirt and tree limbs as it hits, feels the hammer blow of the air again, the slicing iciness of the snow as it covers him, the soft ride down the mountain. He remembers being stupid with cold.

I really have come back from the dead, he thinks to himself. Nothing can hurt me anymore. He looks around at his ruined kitchen, at the dish marks on the walls, and at the shards under his feet. He looks with love and joy at the broken and battered surfaces, and then he realizes, with wonder, that he hasn't come back from the dead at all, that he's still with them. He realizes he can no longer touch the living, with their obsessions with the past and their worries about the future, their whining and their gossip, their concern with getting old and sick and alone. He will walk through their world as a wraith, touching its bright colors with longing and wonder and from a distance, with a caress so soft it cannot be felt. Women will know him only as a ghost, a fragment of dream, a demon who comes to them in the night, and mornings will always throw their memory of him and even his existence itself into doubt. Babies will cry and dogs will howl when he walks through a room.

He laughs. Death seems to be a sly joke, a smirky distillation of the truth of his life and the lives of lovers and friends, an ironic crystallization of what Suzanne called his inability to grow up. Death has been with him all his life, he thinks, and only now has chosen to show Itself.

He takes off his socks and wades into the water on his kitchen floor, gathering up shards of glass as he goes. It's hard to see underneath the surface and he steps on a sharp edge and cuts his heel. Blood drifts across the floor, and he looks at it over the pile of glass in his palms, delighted at its color, and at the swirls it makes in the water, and at the slow drift it takes toward the stairs.

NIGHTWIND

AT SUNSET THAT NIGHT A LINE OF ice-blue clouds came over Mount Mammon, trailing long streamers of snow that hid the trees and the ski lift towers and the yellowed grass of the ski runs. I walked downtown and began looking for a bar that was warm and not too crowded. Lots of people were back in town already, driving around with new skis on top of their new cars, trying to hurry the season. They think they're going to live forever.

I found a place that had a free table near the front and was sitting at it with a beer when Ackerman came through the door. Right behind him was Sandra, my best friend in this town. She looked at me and grinned and shrugged.

Ackerman and I shared a room in the employee dorm during the 1974-75 season, when I was washing dishes at the lodge dining room and he was a first-year ski instructor. After the season he started selling organic skin products for one of those suck-your-neighbors-in pyramid organizations. Then he got into vitamins and protein diet powders. Then he married a girl he met while selling wood stoves and they bought a house in suburb outside of Babylon. That's where they live now, heating with gas and eating at fast-food places and making payments on a pre-owned Mercedes SL. When he's on his selling trips Ackerman drives a VW van.

He stopped in front of my table and said, "I thought I'd find you in a bar."

"I like bars," I said. And I do.

"I found her in a bar across the street," he said, pointing at Sandra.

"She likes bars, too."

"I saw her across the room. She saw me. I had never seen her looking more beautiful. I thought she was a goddess. A divine spark passed between us."

Sandra didn't say anything. She's not divine. And she's not beautiful. She looks a lot like my sister would have looked if I'd had a sister, which means in some lights she's not even pretty. But she is a decent human being. Sometimes Ackerman has no idea what he's saying to people.

"We're in love," said Ackerman, and sat down across from me. "We're going to be married."

"You can't," I said. "You're already married. I went to your wedding, remember?"

"I would never have invited you if I'd known you were going to get drunk and tell the world about it."

"I'm not drunk," I said. And I wasn't.

"You invited me, too," said Sandra. She pulled a chair from another table and sat down between us.

Ackerman shrugged. "So I made a mistake. It wasn't the only one I made that day." He looked at me like it was my fault.

"What are you pushing these days, anyway?" I asked him.

He grinned. "Solar-powered organic greenhouses. You can grow anything in them. Twenty-pound tomatoes. Potatoes that get mistaken for small ponies. Kiwi fruit you go bowling with. Cucumbers...."

"Don't get started on cucumbers," said Sandra.

"Giant, green, firm cucumbers," said Ackerman.

"Right," said Sandra. "A purple shade of green."

"Cucumbers that throb with vegetable life," said Ackerman. "Cucumbers you can worship. Cucumbers...."

"What's this lead up to?" I asked Sandra.

"An invitation to go out to his van and see his brochures."

"Did you go?" I asked.

She shook her head. "It's cold out there in the parking lot. And the night's still young. And I was afraid he was really serious about selling me a greenhouse."

"Go ahead. Laugh at me if you want," said Ackerman. "You know what's on supermarket produce? Pesticides. You know

28

what happens when you ingest pesticides? Lymphoma, that's what happens. Scientific studies prove it. Lym*phoma*."

"No high-pressure sales tactics here," said Sandra.

The cocktail waitress came by.

Ackerman pointed at my beer. "Time to get the evening moving. We'll have three scotches. On the rocks. I'm buying," he said, and handed her a bill. "That's a fifty, not a twenty."

He looked the waitress up and down as she turned and went back to the bar.

"She's beautiful," he said. "Isn't she?"

"I don't know," I said.

"C'mon. She's a goddess. Give me a number. On a scale from one to ten, what is she?"

"Ask Sandra," I said.

Sandra looked over at the bar. "She *is* beautiful. She might even be a goddess. Probably the only goddess in town. She's at least an eight or a nine, Ackerman."

"No," said Ackerman. "Nowhere near a nine. She's three drinks away from a nine." He peered across at me. "Of course, she could still be the only goddess in town," he said.

"The Goddess of Scotch," said Sandra.

"Queen of the Hops," I said, wishing Ackerman had just ordered me another beer.

Ackerman turned away from us and looked down the bar, all the way to the back, and said, "Nobody's left here from 1974. Do you know how many people I've recognized tonight?"

"None," I said.

"Not none," he said. He looked back at me, irritated. "Three. Sandra and you and now that waitress. I've seen her every time I've been in town for the last fifteen years. She doesn't recognize me. She never recognizes me. She's a goddess and to her I'm just another drunken asshole."

"Goddesses are psychic," I said.

"Psychic has nothing to do with it. You look like a drunken asshole to her, too. Ask her. Go up to her and say, 'Do I look like anything but a drunken asshole to you?' "

Sandra giggled. "Don't risk it."

"See," said Ackerman. "Sandra's the only one of us who doesn't look like some out-of-town, away-from-the-wife-and-kids, ass-grabbing salesman who's had too much to drink and too much pain in his life and who wants her to fix it all for him."

"A speech," I said.

"I'm not even done. Do you know that Sandra is the only one of us who has any chance of achieving an honest, human, intimate relationship with that woman?"

"I thought she was a goddess," I said.

"To you and me, he said, "she is. We have this spiritual need to worship her in her bunk tonight. But she looks at Sandra, she sees something else."

"Sandra's a decent human being."

"I'm a decent human being, too," said Ackerman.

"But what I really want to be is an asshole," said Sandra.

"Good luck," said Ackerman. He didn't say it nicely.

The waitress returned with the drinks.

"How would you," Ackerman said to her, "like a a great deal on a solar-powered, completely self-contained, highly organic greenhouse?"

"I don't have room for one in my apartment," she said, and handed him the change from his fifty.

"You need one badly and don't even know it," Ackerman said. "Nurturing little baby green things can make you a much better person."

"Who is this asshole?" the waitress asked me.

"Some guy from out of town." I said. "A salesman. Watch your back around him. He's away from his wife and kids."

"I knew I'd seen him before," she said.

"That wasn't funny," said Ackerman when she left.

Sandra laughed. "It was funny, Ackerman."

Ackerman only looked at her, wounded.

"Maybe you had to be there," she said, and got up and walked to the restroom.

Ackerman gestured at her. "Same old Sandra. You'd have thought she might have got a little better looking with time."

"She doesn't worry about her looks all that much," I said.

"No kidding. She should, though. A little makeup, a little

work on her hair, some clothes that let people know she's not a bag lady—she'd be okay, you know?"

Then he said, "I'm going to see if she wants to go dancing across the street. You mind?"

"Why should I?"

"I thought you two were old friends."

"We are," I said. "We're just not old dance partners."

"That's right," he said. "I forgot. You don't dance. You just sit."

He asked me how the skiing had been over last winter. I told him fine, but I thought my knees were going because they clicked and popped and hurt every time I bent them anymore. He said he had lost touch with the town, and that he was going to take a winter off sometime and go skiing with me. I told him he should. He's a good skier. The best times I've ever had with him were when we were skiing. We'd had this conversation before.

When Sandra got back to the table he asked her if she wanted to go dancing. She did. She downed the rest of her drink and told Ackerman she was ready to go.

"Stay here," said Ackerman to me. "Don't move. We'll be right back."

It was still snowing outside and when they opened the door I could see that it was beginning to pile up on the sidewalk.

"Be nice to the nice waitress," said Ackerman.

The waitress came back with another drink. "The lady bought you one," she said.

"Thank you," I said. "Thank you very much."

She gave me a fixed smile and turned away from me. It could have been that she was having a bad night. Even goddesses must have bad nights sometime.

Then I began to wonder if it would be possible to sit all night in the bar and drink and say thank you quietly and politely, in tones of worship, and finally impress her, this immortal, this eight or nine or whatever she was, with what a decent human being I was. Probably not. Just about the time she would look at me with hope in her eyes, I'd fall off my stool and go to sleep on the floor.

Anyway, even if Ackerman was right and she was a goddess, she was still a goddess that served alcohol for a living. Her hope wouldn't be that she had finally found a decent human being—goddesses aren't much impressed with decent human beings, I don't think—but that it was getting close to closing time and if I'd just leave she could clean up and go home. Some situations you lose anyway you play them, and yearning after a goddess is one of them.

But then I began to think that sometime, somewhere, in a bar far, far away, there must have been a cocktail waitress who looked at one of her customers with the same sort of yearning for the divine that she had sparked in maybe fifty ordinary human beings that evening. She would have told him to wait, and given him a free drink now and then until the bar was cleaned up. Then she would have said to him, as they walked out the door after closing time, "Let's go to my place. Olympus is so beautiful in the morning."

I had been imagining myself as that suddenly extraordinary human being—that extraordinarily decent human being—for awhile and wondering if there was some simple chant I could repeat to make it all happen when Sandra sat down beside me.

"That was quick," I said.

She sighed. "He's selling a greenhouse to a woman bartender. He's got her cornered behind the bar and she can't get away."

"Did you dance?"

"The band is between sets." Sandra was angry. Ackerman does that to women. Put a woman around Ackerman, and sooner or later she'll get pissed off. I thought of what Ackerman's wife was doing right then, and an image came to me of her driving his Mercedes around Babylon in the dark, picking up hitchhikers.

"He'll be back as soon as the band starts," I said.

"Too late," said Sandra. The waitress came by and she ordered another scotch.

"Just once," said Sandra, "I would like to be that good-looking."

"You're good looking," I said.

"No I'm not. Not like that. I'm not so good looking that anyone would ever sit alone in here and buy drinks so they could maybe talk to me and maybe pick me up and maybe take me home. Even if it was my job to be nice to people so the last thing I would do is be nice to anyone for free."

I smiled at her. Sandra has a way of keeping things honest.

"So what would you do if you were that good looking?" I asked her.

"It's what I wouldn't do. I wouldn't treat Ackerman like a human being. I wouldn't go dancing with him. I wouldn't pay any attention to him at all."

"She's already doing that for you. It drives him crazy."

"Just once I'd like to be able to drive somebody crazy."

"That's an ambition that's beneath you." And it was true. She was better than that. It came to me quite suddenly then that it's better to be human than divine. Decently human, that is.

"You always say the nicest things," Sandra said. "I wish they were always true." She stood up. "Let's get out of here before he comes back."

I gave the waitress ten dollars for Sandra's drink and told her to keep the change and that she could have the drink for herself, if she wanted it. I was very careful not to look her in the eyes and I said good night like it was a prayer, hoping my tone would indicate we appreciated her services and we liked her bar and had been wonderfully happy while we were in it, so happy that we now arose to do her will in the world.

The waitress looked at me like I was possessed, shrugged, and stuffed the money into her tip tray. I told myself if I ever met her anyplace besides her bar, I would introduce myself and ask her if she was doing anything that evening. It would be morning and I would be looking almost healthy in the sunlight and she would instantly know that I was a decent human being.

Then I thought there must have been a time, back in the bright morning of the world, when human beings were just finding that fermented honey could make them see the shimmer of gods in each other's faces, when temples were bars and cocktail waitresses were priestesses, and you could go down to your corner temple and have a few quick glasses of mead and come out feeling like a more decent human being than you had been when you went in. Because when you reached for the glass, your fingertips would dance with those of a woman who, on her shift anyway, really was a goddess, who wore a golden mask and who looked out of it with eyes that saw the world and your place in it, and neither of those things lacked wonder. The tips of your fingers, I thought again, would dance.

After I had thought this I looked at the waitress and I wanted to brush fingertips with her, but I couldn't do it just by accident. If I did it on purpose she would think I was just another drunken asshole and then I couldn't, for reasons of dignity, go back in that bar for a long, long time.

As it was, I followed Sandra out the door. When I got out on the sidewalk I didn't see her right away because the snow was still coming down. Then I saw she had gone to a streetlight and was standing under it. She looked small and pale and terribly human and I knew that I could touch her when and where I wanted but I thought I might start with her fingertips. Sandra was holding her shoulders and had her head down. I thought she was crying but as I got close to her she seemed all right.

"You just gave our waitress ten bucks for a drink I didn't drink," she said. "You think that finally impressed her?"

"I thought it would impress you," I said.

"It did," she said. "That was breakfast."

We began walking. After half a block, Sandra said she wanted me to go home with her even if I had given my money away.

"You sure you don't want to try your luck across the street?" I wondered about Sandra on the dance floor, and wondered if now and then, she didn't catch glimpses of gods among the dancers.

"I'm in the mood for a sure thing," she said. Then, as an afterthought, she said, "And a decent human being."

"You always say the nicest things," I said.

We turned a corner and began walking toward her apartment. A cold old powerful wind was coming down her street from off of Mammon, carrying heavier, sharper snowflakes, ones that rushed and bit at our faces, and then, just as suddenly, went on into the night.

SHADOWMAN

IMAGINE THIS: A MAN IN BLACK SNAKE-skin, tip-toeing through your neighborhood on moonless nights, lying still as death against the dark edges of houses, under fences, behind trees, running madly from shadow to shadow. His face is hidden by a mask, his hands by dark leather. From a dozen points he watches a bright unshaded window—yours, perhaps. Imagine, if you can, the concentration of his thoughts on what is behind the glass. While you're reaching in the closet for your shotgun, think of the unbridgeable gulf between that man and you. What is he doing out there? Why would he want to peer into your life?

And imagine: The same man by day, a mild-mannered and suffering—who knows? A realtor, maybe, with some property of his own he's trying to unload, and a dozen or so other houses he's trying to sell for anxious and demanding clients. His kids take drugs, his car makes a tooth-grinding howl the dealer can't seem to fix, and his wife has just run off to be with the infamous Tibetan Sage of the New Age, the guru Toko-Ra.

So imagine this realtor as a man of forty, a little overweight, with scale-prints on the unsunned skin of his belly, and darkness in the moons under his eyes. He's sleepy and he finds it hard to concentrate. At times, going over a contract or showing a house, the thought comes to him that This Cannot Go On, or I Can't Stand It Anymore, but the This and the It are things not well defined in his mind. They are functions, mostly, of the sleep-ridden pain he's feeling. He is not much of an associative thinker, or he'd figure out that running around all night and peeping in windows will eventually cut into his commissions.

But you—you have learned to be an associative thinker. You make connections. You keep your eyes and ears open, your thoughts moving.

You've even thought about the guru Toko-Ra, whose commune this guy's wife has joined. You've watched him on TV, this laughing decadent therapist to fugitive housewives, who drives a dozen Lamborghinis and who promises hassle-free sex and relationships that magically transform loneliness into solitude.

Toko-Ra is said to be behind the breakup of thousands of marriages, although you suspect that many of the women who flock to his Wyoming ranch and his elite corps of six-and-a-half-foot cowhands are fleeing dull married life as much as they are seeking anything. Some of them, you've heard, have forgone the cowhands and become ranch nuns, have taken vows of celibacy and silence and have assumed control of alfalfa production, and of eggs. You've made jokes about relationships with chickens, or hay. You have made jokes about people who think loneliness can be transformed into anything at all.

But you imagine this guy's wife anyway, an understimulated and lonely woman who must have said to herself, as she fixed yet another dinner for clients or as she dutifully searched her children's dresser drawers for perspective-changing substances: This Cannot Go On. I Can't Stand It Anymore. Then, intuiting something beyond a husband who watched TV but otherwise dealt with material reality as though it were the only reality, the wife of the man in snakeskin turned away from home, hearth, and family, packed her bag and set out for the spiritual Tetons, the Yellowstone Country of the soul.

You look toward your own wife, her dishwashing done, her floors swept and waxed, her beds made, her children banished to their rooms to do homework or to listen to heavy-metal music or to smoke something in the closet or to do whatever it is that children do at night: she, this wife of yours, is sitting in the rocking chair you bought her, her face bright with video-light, rapt, attentive, for a moment laughing. You are grateful for her sanity and wonder: Why Is It That Some Women Go Crazy and Others Stay Okay? She works, too. Sometimes in a bank, sometimes in a law office. She types. She takes dictation. My Wife, you think. Think I'll Hang On To Her, you think.

But there's still the problem of the guy outside your window, invisible, wifeless, who had to have been massively bummed when he came home expecting a cold drink and a hot meal and instead got a note: Keep the Kids, Keep the Car, Keep the House and All The Other Material Plane Illusions. We Must All Follow Our Paths. Even Bad Shit Causes Us To Grow. Love, she signed it.

Maybe it's a long way from that moment to running around in too-tight clothes—it's not really snakeskin, it's bio-patterned Lycra, popular among athletes whose endorphin addiction has reached terminal proportions—anyway, running around in too-tight clothes, peeking in night-lit windows, being the very picture of a community exile—it's whole light years, you might say, from that moment of New Age divorce to this one of total Dark Age loneliness, solitude, alienation, whatever—but you know he got there somehow. A tangential question: Whatever happened to those dopey guys, Sonny Bono and Ike Turner and Marilyn Monroe's first husband, guys who never figured out they had married women half-divine? (Remember Sonny and Cher? Ike and Tina?)

That shadow you think you see moving out in the darkness might be like those men, each of whom had a moment of crisis, too, when the woman he called wife was forever separated from him by a veil of light. Did those guys wake up? Did they heed the call for a new and improved kind of Male Consciousness?

Of course it's not quite the same with the guy in your yard. His wife just got herself a guru, she didn't become a superstar. So he has been under no real imperative to wake up, or even to realize a man can go through life in a state of cultural sleep. He can just go about his business of selling properties and putting his kids through college and he won't be bothered with people asking him Hey Fella Would You Have Slapped Her Around If You'd Known She'd Be Running Thunderdome?

Still, when she was out the door it had to be like an alarm clock going off in his head, and he couldn't just reach in and hit the snooze button. He must have wondered: can a woman just up and leave her husband and family for no reason at all? Don't women value relationships more than men? Don't they cherish men who set out to be a good husband and father, who work, who don't drink to excess or run around? What possible lack could she have felt?

And how could she have thrown him into a world that he had so safely insulated himself from? For awhile, there, he was immune to the lonesome wiles of the women who buy big houses with divorce settlements. He couldn't dream of going off to some exotic beach with somebody newer, firmer, more beautiful, because he was, after all, a family man with the beginnings of a weight problem, with a mortgage and kids and a wife who up to now had uncomplainingly loved him. He had begun the process of transferring personal hopes and ambitions to his offspring. He had prided himself on knowing when to settle down and run easy in the harness. He had prided himself on living in the Real World.

But then she had run off with Toko-Ra, an event which had made him suddenly vulnerable to a loneliness he hadn't known he had the capacity for, and his world vulnerable to an ephemerality he had never before associated with stone and wood and glass. He found himself having long talks with divorcées in the master bedrooms of unsold houses, asking questions about women of women who were in no shape to give him answers. He began lusting after his babysitters, and asking them on road trips. Some of them laughed. None of them accepted.

He had gotten depressed. A doctor recommended exercise—running, specifically—as a way to relieve stress. He had bought the outfit: shoes, tights, shorts, Walkman, various logoed T-shirts. And he had begun to make tentative trips around town, jogging and walking. He had not noticed how stuck in the world his body had become until he began trying to move it.

But he kept at it, and there was an evening when he stepped into his tights and the feeling was electric, erotic even, akin to the excitement he had felt when, as a pre-teen, he had opened a new Spiderman or Legion of Super Heroes Comic. The Lycra was a bit rounder around him than it was around most superheroes, but that didn't matter. His slide into Spandex generated magnetic fields that bent space, twisted time back on itself, brought him safely home to that long-lost, comic-book-reading Self.

—And left him in the grip of adolescent longings, frightening desires that had nothing to do with making money or selling houses or being a good husband or father. He smelled musk in the air, heard the heart-homing rush of blood in his veins, remembered foolish dreams of hang-gliding or free climbing or floating through Canada to the Arctic Ocean. Once he had wanted to sail, in a small boat, alone and complete—to Bali, to Burma, to unnamed islands in the Andaman Sea.

And they are foolish dreams, aren't they? Sitting in your comfortable home, shotgun in hand, waiting for a quick tiny movement out there so you can blast away at it while it's still on your property and a legal kill, you know, if you know anything at all, that they are very foolish dreams. They corrode a man's links to the world. Dream them and the landscape of your life will become flat desert, dull and poverty-stricken and starved.

QUICK! THERE HE IS! Run to the sliding glass door, throw it open, thrust the muzzle of your shotgun out into darkness. Pull the trigger—no, it's gone. It was the flash of far carlight on your garbage can. A neighbor's dog howls. You shut the door. Your wife looks up from the Letterman program. "What is it?" she asks. You have no words to give her. She turns back to the TV. With a shock, you realize she is used to seeing you walk around the house with a gun.

Which is fine. A man's got a right to defend his property. And out there, there's a guy who has been getting closer and closer to some very slippery edge—partly because Lycra comes in shades of black. It isn't all hot pink and turquoise. An image has taken shape in that guy's mind, something born of long-repressed Comic Needs. Every glowing spring day he has spent in his cramped office, every rational decision and every mature sacrifice he's made—all these have created a vacuum in his life, one that has sucked up all the hormonal urges and forbidden hopes and unworthy wants he has ever had. And these have assembled beyond his personal event horizon into a vaguely human form that—Voila!—looks at him every evening from the mirror.

Urged on by clerks in sports stores, he has purchased higher and higher-tech running shoes, heartbeat monitors, fingerless gloves, glowing stopwatches, headset radios. Standing in full-length glittering snakeskin, LEDs blinking, staring into the silvered glass at the end of his closet, he finally recognizes the entity he has conjured up: SHADOWMAN.

Hey, Hey. Hey, Hey. A mild-mannered and sleepy realtor by day, but by night? Look out. Because he's the Defender of the Dark, Guardian of the Glimmer, Strongman of the Subliminal, Demigod of the Dream—he's the tick of a settling house, the brush of branch against a window, the faint drip-drip-drip of a forever leaky faucet. He's the quick thrill of endo-amphetamine at the approach of the full moon, the unheard noise that breaks a sound sleep, the snap of the hypnotist's fingers, the—.

But wait. Is Shadowman Superhero or Supervillain? There would be no doubt in your mind, of course, even if he wasn't wearing a mask. You're going to shoot the creep if you catch him.

And the police, if they find him hiding in one of your trees instead of staying in the street and maintaining the proper level of a-erobic exercise, they'll work him over a little bit, handcuff him and shove his head, bang, against the patrol car roof, and take him down to the station. He'll be charged with voyeurism or trespassing and will end up in the News of Record along with other unfortunates who didn't pay their bills or drove drunk or punched out a bouncer. And if your neighbors see him, they'll sic their dogs on him. And if the people who are anxiously waiting for him to sell their houses find out what he does at night, they'll cancel their contracts and mutter cynically about real estate agents as a group.

There are only a few people on the planet who might understand what he's become. Sonny Bono. Ike Turner. Marilyn Monroe's dopey first husband.

And the infamous New Age Tibetan guru Toko-Ra, who would greet him gleefully, happily, as one greets an equal, a much-valued sharer of perspective. Severed from his daytime multiple-listed identity, Shadowman would be made welcome in the shadow of the Tetons, honored by a full turn-out of staff, given his own his ranch-nun chauffeured Lamborghini, encouraged to laugh at himself, and told to rejoice in his own alienation. You have escaped a culture that is sick, Toko-Ra would tell him.

Toko-Ra has actually told evil lies like this to people who have given up perfectly decent lives to follow him.

A movement catches the corner of your eye. It's your wife's rocking chair, swinging forward and back. She's gone upstairs to check the kids or has gone to bed. A sudden thought disturbs you. She seems to have been getting a lot smaller lately, and you wonder if the process hasn't suddenly accelerated, and she's become microbe-sized right there in front of the TV. She might be stuck down in the weave of the upholstery right now, lost forever.

Oh, God. Where do thoughts like that come from? You get a sudden unbidden picture of multiple bits of yourself, in small leaky vessels atop a black sea. The Boat People of the Mind. Don't think those things, you tell yourself. They are Not Acceptable Thoughts. Stop them right now.

You go to the window to lower the blinds and go to bed. Tomorrow is another day. You've got properties to look at, contracts to prepare. But the questions still come nagging, and they're not about anything you'll be doing in the morning: What's Really Out There In The Dark? What Does It Want From YOU?

Without willing it, you see yourself framed in a small, square box of light, backgrounded by floral wallpaper, surrounded by an overstuffed couch, wildlife prints on the walls, brass lamps, oriental rug, flickering TV and stilled rocking chair. It's a scene redundantly snug and cozy and normal.

And because you're an associative thinker, you see that small, homey scene through Shadowman's condemned-to-be-superhuman eyes, see it as that real world that you occupy and he cannot. You know, suddenly, that his eyes lovingly and sadly caress the normal. He is watching a kind of video, you realize, the way that children of divorce watch the middle-class TV families, pitting their knowledge of the world against the screen's fantasy, and for a while, letting the fantasy win. Another Unacceptable Thought.

You grasp the cord to lower the blinds and there—What? OH, GOD, NO! There, in the glass of the door, the image of a man, darkened almost to invisibility, eyes glinting in the depths of their sockets, standing right in front of you, mouth open, howling something, trying to come in, trying to reach you—.

And you raise the shotgun and fire. There is a flash and a deafening roar. Shadowman is shattered into a million spinning, flashing shards. Holes appear in your garbage cans. A stray dog, sniffing through your flower garden, screams one agonized scream, then yelps his way down the street.

And nothing is outside, except a cold dark breeze that makes its way into your living room and pushes the rocking chair back and forth, back and forth, back and forth. Your ears are ringing. Faint laughter comes from the TV. There is no other sound. You put down the gun and walk slowly to the stairs, to begin the search for your wife.

POST COWBOY DREAMS

A HARD RAIN CAME OVER MOUNT
Mammon and onto Gomorrah, soaking the hot bleached grass of
backyards and turning the gutters in the middle of town into small
rivers carrying beer cans, styrofoam cups, and crumpled Bible
Days programs. Bicyclists began pedaling for coffee shops. Down
in the city park, a city-league softball game, rugby practice and a
pick-up game of basketball were all rained out.

And in the middle of Main Street, Sonny Cogan, who should
have been glad it was raining, was instead cursing, trying to get his
horse turned around and off the water-slick asphalt. His hat was
starting to feel soggy. Rain was oozing through his Levi jacket and
into his new cowboy shirt. A car went by too close, spraying an
even band of mud across the horse and Sonny's pantleg.

The horse jumped and turned and made a little experimental
hop toward the curb. Then it started bucking for real, but Sonny
was already out of the saddle and into the air. He landed on his
feet just as the horse slipped and fell to its knees. As it struggled to
get up, he jumped back in the saddle and pulled hard on the reins,
screaming, "Buck, you nervous son of a bitch. Buck!" He pulled
the reins up until the horse started jerking backward, fighting the
pain of the bit, blowing hard.

Sonny backed the horse across the street, stopping traffic. The
drivers of motorhomes began honking their horns. The horse
flinched and jumped. Sonny kept its head high and raked its flanks
with his spurs. It reared again, and touched the far curb with its
rear hooves. Sonny released the reins, and when the horse
touched down, he whirled it around and onto the sidewalk, right
into the middle of a Japanese tour group that was standing under
the awning of The Slaver's Rest Saloon.

They scattered. Sonny could hear the clicking of Nikons and

shouts of "Cow Boy! Cow Boy!" and "Shanecomeback. Shanecomeback!"

Sonny eased the reins and the horse, wild-eyed, stood on the slick concrete, legs wide and trembling. He dismounted to applause. Sonny doffed his hat and bowed to them in the way he'd been taught by the representative of the Japanese Consul at the Chamber of Commerce meeting. Then, showing off, he led the horse over to a parking meter and tied the reins to it and put a quarter in the slot. He undid the cinch and pulled the saddle and blankets off and leaned them against the wall underneath the awning, out of the rain.

"Watch he doesn't kick somebody's head off," he said to the Japanese.

"Cow Boy!" they said.

Sonny pulled open the heavy door of The Rest. It was dark and silent and empty inside. He stood for a moment, letting his eyes adjust to the reduced light, then remembered and took off his sunglasses. Jimmy the Bartender looked up, saw him, and without words poured a beer for him. Sonny sat down.

"Raining out there," said Jimmy. "Hard."

Sonny didn't say anything. He looked at Jimmy for a long moment, then took off his hat, shook a fine spray of water off it, and placed it on the bar to one side of him.

Jimmy shrugged. "You work in a bar with no windows," he said, "and you have to get your weather reports from the humidity of your customers."

Sonny still didn't say anything. He sipped from his beer and stared off into the dark corners of the bar. He was the only customer. Most people didn't show up in The Rest until after dark.

"How's business?" asked Jimmy.

"Dirty," said Sonny. "Dust six inches deep on the trails."

"Rain help?" asked Jimmy.

"Mud tomorrow," said Sonny. "Dust the day after." He shrugged. "It ain't so bad. I get to ride in front."

He stared deep into his beer, watching strings of bubbles. "Today my clients were twelve little kids. I rode them around the loop behind the stables until they all had a nice even coat of dust. Couldn't tell them apart. When their parents got there, they'd point out one that looked a little familiar, and I'd get on my horse and cut him out of the herd."

Sonny thought of his horses in the pasture north of town. He had turned them loose an hour before and had looked on as they had bucked and snorted their way through the sagebrush toward the river. Watching them, he had thought it might rain, but he'd ridden into town anyway, on a skittish new horse. Now his new cowboy shirt was wet. He put his beer on the bar and took off his jacket. Water had soaked into the piping of the shirt and had carried little blue stains into the silk, making it look tie-dyed.

"It could rain for the next forty days and nights," said Sonny, "and I wouldn't care."

"Season over?" asked Jimmy.

"Soon," said Sonny. "A couple of weeks and I'll take the horses to fall pasture."

"Where's that?"

"South. In-laws own some ranches down there."

"In-laws?" asked Jimmy. "Thought you were divorced."

Sonny nodded. "Ex-in-laws. They still like me, though. I still pay them money. They still winter my horses."

"Maybe they just like your horses."

"Maybe. But her brother tells me not to worry about any hard feelings on his part. He says it's nothing personal. It's just that I don't have what she wants."

"Nothing personal," said Jimmy.

"It's true," said Sonny. "I don't have what she wants. I don't think the man's been made who has what she wants. She's been gone a year now, and unless I've missed somebody, she's run with four different carpenters. And a real estate developer. Her ski instructor. And some kid who lets her snort his cocaine and ride his motorcycle."

Jimmy nodded. "She brings them in now and then. Not all at once, though. You say you did finally get divorced?"

"It was final last week," said Sonny. He grinned at Jimmy. "That tell you anything about the weather?"

Jimmy grinned back. "That it hasn't rained in years," he said. "That tumbleweeds are blowing down Main Street, and all the windows in all the houses are dark and frosted with fly shit."

Two women came through the door with bicycles, dripping water. Sonny thought of his string, by now huddled under the big trees on the river bank. The new horse outside was probably not enjoying the weather on Main Street, but he would be all right. Dude horses had to learn to put up with a lot.

"Lovely creatures, aren't they?" said Jimmy.

"Horses?"

Jimmy pointed. "Women."

"I like them," said Sonny, not turning to look.

Jimmy laughed. "You sure pick some winners."

"I even like the winners," said Sonny.

The women sat down on the two stools next to Sonny. The one closer to him said her name was Kim. The other one was Janice.

"Call me Sonny," said Sonny.

"Is that your horse outside?" asked Kim.

Sonny nodded. "One of them," he said.

"You mind bikes in here?" Janice asked Jimmy.

"We serve anybody," said Jimmy. "Long as their money's good."

"BIKES," said Kim.

"Their money's no good," said Sonny, putting a bill on the bar. "Take it out of this."

"Thanks, cowboy," said Kim.

"It's a pleasure, ma'am," said Sonny, and he picked up his hat and placed it over his heart.

Kim and Janice wanted vodkas with a twist. They were flight attendants, they said, and had both been to Russia, and that was where they had learned to like vodka.

"It was either that or drink the water," said Kim.

"Those people over there," said Janice, "are unlucky. Very unlucky."

"They'll do anything for a pair of blue jeans," said Kim.

"What's your horse's name?" asked Janice.

"Don't have a name," said Sonny. "What will those people over there do for a pair of blue jeans?"

"Anything," said Kim. "Take you around Moscow. Give you their AK-47. Marry you."

"They only want to marry you," said Janice, "to get out of Russia. What do you mean your horse doesn't have a name?"

"He just don't have a name," said Sonny. "Ain't named him."

"A horse has got to have a name," said Kim.

"Did you get yourself an AK-47?" asked Sonny.

"You can't take them on the plane," said Kim. "Even when you work on the plane. I got taken around Moscow instead."

"So what are you going to name your horse?" asked Janice.

"Ain't."

"Aint? What kind of a name is that?"

"Ain't gonna name him."

"A horse has got to have a name," said Kim again.

"You name him, then," said Sonny. "He's just a dude horse."

"George?" asked Kim.

"Already got a horse named George," said Sonny.

"How many horses do you have?" asked Kim.

"Call him Dude," said Janice.

"Fourteen," said Sonny. "Call him what?"

"Dude," said Janice.

"Dude the Horse," said Jimmy the Bartender. "It does have a ring to it."

"That's good," said Sonny. "Dude he is."

"How'd you get fourteen horses?" asked Kim.

"I'm an outfitter," said Sonny. "I sell horse rides. You show up tomorrow morning, I'll let you ride for free."

"I want to ride Dude," said Janice.

"You can't," said Kim. "We've got a charter flight to work tomorrow. You know that."

"Let's ride tonight, then," said Janice.

"It's raining," said Kim.

"I bet it's stopped," said Janice. She jumped off her bar stool and walked to the door. When she pushed it open, sunlight came streaming in, blinding them all.

"C'mon," said Janice. "Let's go tell Dude his name."

Kim jumped off her stool. "She's crazy about horses," she said. "And she's never even been on one."

"Can we ride him?" asked Janice.

"No," said Sonny. "And stay away from his heels."

"I used to have a horse," said Kim. Then she looked at Sonny. "You married, cowboy?"

"Was once," said Sonny. "It was the only way I could get out of Russia."

"I had a horse for two years," said Kim. "Then my parents got a divorce and they sold him. It broke my sixteen-year-old heart. That was ten years ago, and I still remember it every day." She turned and walked to Janice, and they disappeared into the light.

When the door had closed behind them, Sonny said, "Every girl has a horse story."

"Even Catherine the Great," said Jimmy.

"No," said Sonny. "They really do. It's like a boy and his dog. A girl and her horse."

"I think she likes cowboys," said Jimmy.

"She just likes horses," said Sonny.

Jimmy put another beer on the bar, took Sonny's money, and rang up the drinks. "I think you better go check on your horse," he said.

"Dude can take care of himself," said Sonny. But a little later he stepped off his stool and walked to the door, shaded his eyes, and opened it. The first thing he noticed was that his saddle was gone. So was his horse. But he looked down the block in time to see it go around the corner in a hard trot, with Kim and Janice bouncing on its back, one up, one down. Sonny shrugged and went back in the bar.

"They've gone for a ride," said Sonny.

"I thought you said they couldn't."

"I did. But it don't matter. Perfectly good women go bad, you get them around horses."

"Horses, too?" asked Jimmy.

"I'll tell you a story," said Sonny.

"While you're waiting for your horse to come back," said Jimmy, and poured him another beer.

"It's a sad story," said Sonny. "My wife had a dream of horses."

"Ex-wife," said Jimmy. "Please. I see guys in here calling their ex-wives their wives, and the next thing I know they're in jail."

"Ex-wife," said Sonny carefully. "But she still dreamed of horses. A whole herd of them. Arabians. And they'd roam over a big ranch full of mountains and meadows, and it would be her ranch, and she'd ride on the whitest Arabian, and she'd ride the world until she found Her Cowboy."

"Are Arabians white?" asked Jimmy.

"These were. Every one of them. Clearcoat metallic white. And maybe they had wings, too. In fact I think they did. Every one of them had wings. They cost a little more that way, but it's worth it on hot days."

"Like Pegasus," said Jimmy. "The horse with wings."

"That's probably where she got the idea," said Sonny. "Off an old gas station sign."

"A whole herd of Pegasuses," said Jimmy.

"Pegasi," said Sonny. "A flock. That's what she wanted." He looked straight at Jimmy, and for a second his mouth became just a scar. "But she was a practical woman. She knew winged horses are rare and hard to catch and aerodynamically suspect anyway. So she decided she would search for Her Cowboy on a regular horse."

"Sounds practical," said Jimmy.

"Because cowboys hang out at rodeos, she learned to barrel race. She became a rodeo queen."

"She was a rodeo queen?"

"The Sodom Stampede. 1972. She never got over it."

"You married a rodeo queen," said Jimmy. "There are worse claims to fame."

"I used to come home," said Sonny, "and catch her in front of the mirror with her queen's outfit on. You know what? She still looks good in hot pink polyester. Snakeskin boots and a black felt hat and a neat little riding whip...." He stared into his own reflection behind the bar. Then he looked at Jimmy, grabbed his hat and put it over his heart again. "I still love that woman," he said.

"Your story," said Jimmy.

"The story," said Sonny, "is that we met at a rodeo. I'd gotten stomped on by a bull and she took pity on me." He put his hat back on. "We met. We married. She thought I was Her Cowboy.

"We leased a little ranch south of town. It was our homestead. I was going to break and train horses. We built corrals together. Bought a brood mare. Bought a stallion. Arabians. Didn't have any wings. But I think she thought we were going to breed them until they did have."

"You make money?" asked Jimmy.

"No," said Sonny. "We lost our asses."

"I thought they were Arabians."

Sonny took a long look at his beer. "This story is more than sad. It's tragic. You should remember that."

"You lost your Arabians."

"And our asses. We had to sell our brood stock. I took the money and bought a dude string and started taking tourists out on trail rides. She took it hard. First the horses didn't grow wings, and then Her Cowboy stopped being a cowboy."

"She didn't really think they were going to grow wings," said Jimmy.

"It's a metaphor," said Sonny.

"Pretty stupid metaphor if you ask me," said Jimmy.

"It's not stupid," said Sonny. "I knew what she was talking about."

"You thought they had wings, too?"

"Once when I was in high school," said Sonny, "I climbed over a fence and jumped on a horse. No saddle, no bridle, no nothing. It was dark. No moon."

"Is this part of the story?"

"Shut up. The horse stood there for a moment. I could feel him breathing under me, the night was so still. I don't think the horse knew he didn't have a saddle or a bridle on. Then I kicked him in the flanks, and he gave a big snort and we took off."

"It was dark?"

"Couldn't see a thing. And it seemed like he ran forever. It was a spring night. Warm and black and feeling like it was about to be full of rain. The best feeling I've ever had. I remember thinking I could die right then and it would be all right."

"You wanted to die on a horse," said Jimmy. "That's a tragic story. A truly tragic story."

"Didn't you ever feel anything you wanted to last forever?" asked Sonny.

"Once," said Jimmy. "It didn't."

"Jimmy," said Sonny, "That night, that horse had wings."

Jimmy picked a beer glass from the rack above his head and stared at it. He grabbed a bar towel and began polishing the water spots off it. Then he put it under the beer tap and carefully filled it. Then he drank from it and put it down in front of him. "That's not tragic," he said. "It's not even sad."

"Wrong. It is tragic. Because after the horse ran and ran that night, and after I felt those great wings on either side of me, and the whole world far below me, and the power of that big wild beating heart between my legs, then we ran into a barbed-wire fence. I was thrown free, and landed on my back in an irrigation canal. I got wet. But the horse broke both front legs."

"Not his wings."

"The wings are a metaphor. Legs are harder to fix."

"So it is a tragic story," said Jimmy. "What's it got to do with your ex-wife?"

"My ex-wife," said Sonny, "doesn't believe in fences. Or tragedy either. If she'd told the story, she'd still be flying up around the moon and you—just because you sat and listened to her—you'd be there with her and you'd be in love with her and the horse would be in love with you both instead of having to be shot because both front legs were broke—because it would have never have hit the fence, and never would have had to be put out of its misery, the way she'd tell it."

"I have not fallen in love in years," said Jimmy.

"How about misery?"

"Misery," said Jimmy, "is an occupational hazard."

"Then you'll understand what it had to feel like when I come home one day and find her putting her stuff in a carpenter's pickup. The carpenter's sitting at the wheel and he won't look at me.

" 'You're not a cowboy,' she tells me when she sees me. 'Cowboys herd cows. You're just a people-boy.'

" 'I'm trying to make a living,' I tell her.

'Running pony rides?' she says. 'Riding little kids off into the sunset while their parents play golf?' Then she says, 'It's just not the great glowing West with you in it.'"

"Nothing personal," said Jimmy.

"It gets worse," said Sonny. " 'Don't leave,' I tell her. 'I love you.'

"She starts crying. 'Damn you,' she says. Then she says, 'I knew you were going to be a shit about this.' And still the carpenter won't look at me."

There was a silence. Finally Jimmy asked, "End of story?"

"Sure," said Sonny.

The door opened. A softer light pooled in front of the doorway. Kim walked in and stood still, her blonde hair glowing until the door swung shut and the dimness of The Rest closed upon her.

"Look," said Jimmy. "A woman. With wings."

"We've lost Janice," Kim said.

"She fall off the horse?" asked Sonny.

"She fell in love with the horse," Kim said. "She's out there now, talking to him. I don't think you'll get him back."

Sonny shrugged. "I can write up a long-term lease, if she wants. Unlimited mileage, and a buy-back option at the end of three years."

"When you talk to her," said Kim, "Don't put it that way."

Janice pushed open the door and walked toward them, with a smile on her face that was like no smile Sonny had ever seen on a flight attendant. She sat down on the stool next to Sonny's and touched him on the arm.

"I like your horse," said Janice. "I want you to take me for a ride."

"I can do that," said Sonny.

"There's a beautiful sunset going on outside," said Janice. "I want to ride off into it."

"Sunset rides are my specialty," said Sonny. "You're in luck."

"You're not in luck," said Kim. "It's going to get dark before you get even halfway to the sunset. And we have a flight tomorrow."

"My horses can see in the dark," said Sonny.

"Anyway, there's a moon," said Jimmy the Bartender.

"That's right," said Sonny. "There is a moon. Which means you can have a moonlight ride. A moonlight ride with a real cowboy. Silhouettes of pine trees and the river rippling silver in the moonlight. A few strums on the ol' git-tar, big ol' mountains with snow on their tops, hoot owls and—"

"Can I ride Dude?" asked Janice.

"You can ride Dude," said Sonny. "Dude is mighty good on moonlight rides."

"Dude is barely broke," said Kim. "He is a nervous son-of-a-bitch. He bucked us off."

"But he didn't mean to," said Janice. "He told me he didn't."

"I can't stand it," said Kim. "You did this to me in Russia, too. You'd never ridden on a tank before, you said. If we miss our flight—"

"It's going to be a warm night with a big moon," said Janice. "Think about it. Riding along with a beautiful animal under you—"

"I'll take you," said Jimmy the Bartender. "Forget the horse."

"It's got to be with a real cowboy," said Janice.

Jimmy grabbed Sonny's hat off the bar and put it on his head. "How's this?" he asked.

"Gimme that," said Sonny, reaching.

"It isn't the same. You're a bartender." said Janice. "You've probably never even been on a horse. I have. Sonny has."

"Goddammit," said Sonny, "gimme my hat."

Jimmy ducked away from Sonny, then took the hat off and put it over his heart. "I luhuvved that woman," he said.

"What woman?" asked Janice.

"Sonny's been telling me about his wife," said Jimmy.

"Ex-wife," said Sonny. "And give me my hat."

Jimmy handed the hat back to Sonny, who brushed dust off it and put it on his head.

"Don't mess with the hat," said Sonny. Then he turned to Janice and pointed off into a dark corner of The Rest. "Out there, west of town, there's a trail that runs up into the mountains, up to a little lake surrounded by big old pine trees. It's a secret place. Found it one day when I was looking for a lost pony. We'll ride up there and build a fire and watch the big moon come up."

"I'll bring the marshmallows," said Kim.

Janice ran her fingertips up and down Sonny's arm. "I like your shirt," she said.

"We'll look at the stars. Gaze into the fire. Lean back against a tree and look up yonder, and wonder if there are people like us on other planets, out there in the Milky Way—"

"That's what you do on moonlight rides?" asked Jimmy. "I never knew that."

"It's in my brochure," said Sonny. "The package includes a genuine Western midnight snack."

"I think I'd like that," said Janice. "I think I'd like that a lot."

Sonny turned to Janice, looked into her face as if he were looking at her for the first time, and ran the tip of his little finger down her neck to her shoulder. She arched her neck in the direction of his hand, closed her eyes, and shivered at him.

"I guess we'll find out," said Sonny.

"Janice," said Kim, "not again."

Janice ignored her. "C'mon, cowboy," she said. She grabbed Sonny by the elbow and pulled him off his barstool. His spurs jingled against the silence. Janice walked him a little way toward the door, stopped, and looked up at him. "You're really tall in those boots," she said. Then she turned toward Kim. "Don't wait up," she said.

She pulled Sonny toward the door. When they reached it, Sonny pulled it open. A silver and rose glow framed Sonny and Janice for a moment. Then the door swung shut behind them, and the only light that Kim and Jimmy could see was after-image.

"Oh, to be a cowboy," said Jimmy.

"It's not the cowboy," said Kim. "It's the horse."

"For a minute there," said Jimmy, "I thought it was the boots."

"Is there really a lake up there?" asked Kim.

"It's not a very big lake," said Jimmy. "More like a pond. And it's going dry."

"I thought so," said Kim.

"And there's only one tree," said Jimmy. "And it's dead. The drought got it."

"And it's not a secret place," said Kim. "Is it?"

"It's got a road to it, if that's what you mean. And you have to build your campfire in one of those little concrete fireplaces the Forest Service put there."

"And Sonny's not a real cowboy," said Kim. "Is he?"

"Originally he's from Pennsylvania," said Jimmy. "Grew up in the suburbs." He poured her another vodka. "On the house," he said.

Kim toasted him. "To a real bartender," she said.

Jimmy smiled. "Sonny believes in himself," he said. "He believes in his own reality. He believes he came West by choice. Bought a horse. Bought a hat. Married a cowgirl. It's part of a story that he thinks he's making up as he goes along."

"Divorced a cowgirl," said Kim.

"Actually, she divorced him," said Jimmy. "But that doesn't matter."

"He's still got the hat," said Kim.

"That's right. And when he sees that pond it still looks like a lake to him. It'll look like a lake to Janice, too."

"I don't think Janice is looking for a lake tonight," said Kim.

"You're right," said Jimmy. "She's looking to belong to a story that has a cowboy and a horse in it. The lake's just a prop."

"So's the cowboy," said Kim.

Jimmy looked at her with respect. It was not a look he often gave customers. "You're right," he said. "It's all props, isn't it? Sonny's got the hat and the boots and the belt buckle the size of a pie plate, and somewhere out by his stables he's got a four-horse trailer and a pickup. Take them away, and what do you have?"

"The horses," said Kim.

"The horses," said Jimmy. "I forgot the horses. But they're props, too. Sonny grew up watching westerns on TV, and the little kids that he takes on rides probably watch the same westerns on their family cable channel, and Janice has probably watched them, too. But out there, when they all ride the trails outside of town and the dust drifts up like hazy dreams from their horses' hooves, and they hear the soft squeak of leather and smell the hot smell of sagebrush and dry pine, and they see dust-matted flanks and a sunset that look like it's a studio set—how could you say that they're not in a kind of movie? That what they're being and doing isn't something made up by some guy writing for television? That what they think is their own story is simply something out of an old cultural textbook, and it was written by somebody else?"

Jimmy stopped and looked at Kim. She was looking across at the dark wall and didn't seem to be paying attention to his words. But he had a lot of time to think during afternoons in The Rest, and sometimes it seemed that if the ideas he came up with during that time weren't important, then there was nothing in his life that was important at all. He shrugged. That was just on sad days. Sometimes there were other days—and other movies, ones involving bartenders and flight attendants. He wondered how he could get her to hang around until closing time.

"But don't you wonder," he said, "if there isn't some original Text, something that began the whole story—some moment, four hundred years ago, when some long-dead gold-seeking Spaniard got tired of chasing runaway horses, and saw, there in the empty Western Desert, three or four of them on a far ridge, and said to hell with it and went back to camp? That there was, in that first tired and angry release of horses that had escaped their corral, the beginning of all our Western lives? Wasn't that the Original Text from which all our stories came?"

Kim turned slowly toward him, as if being pulled away from a movie screen full of horses that were swift and sleek and beautiful and hers.

"You ever been on a horse?" she asked him.

When Jimmy confessed that he hadn't, she asked, "Then who's this guy Tex anyway?"

SON OF BANSHEE

AH, SPRINGTIME. SEASONAL AFFECTIVE Disorder has disappeared for yet another year. Mongo is biking around town, cruising broken sidewalks, following the shortest possible route to the Gomorrah Taco Time. Sunshine's popping leaves out on the trees above his head. He can smell new grass, damp earth, mushrooms, daffodils, and the warm rot of old wet wood.

Mongo's become a regular at Taco Time, but it's not because of the food. He's in love with a big voluptuous girl who works the lunch shift, and today—if he finally gets up the nerve—he's going to ask her what she's doing after her afternoon classes at the high school. He doesn't see that his being thirty-seven years old is any problem. He knew high school girls who were going out with thirty-seven year old men when he was in high school. It seemed like they all were, in fact.

Mongo, thinking for the third time this week that today might be the day he wins the love lottery, speeds up, turns a corner, and—UH-OH. WHAT'S THIS? A parade, with banners, placards, and pictures, marching feet, and—what?—they're MIDGETS— chanting a twisted singsong mantra like a bunch of Buddhist banshees: NO JUST SAY NO JUST SAY NO JUST SAY NO JUST SAY NO JUST SAY—.

He stops his bike, because even though he's been off hallucinogens for—let's see, maybe a year now, maybe two—Flashbacks Happen. These little people might be personal property, small interior buddies marching over his retinas on their way to more vital organs.

But no—this one's on the outside, he's almost positive. It's a real parade, with real midgets. The midgets get closer, and Mongo sees they've got these big regular-sized people behind them, moving them along the street like shepherds do sheep. Mongo's thinking it's some sort of Midget Halfway House on a field trip, singing midget fight songs and looking for bugs and pond water and pine cones to take back for midget show-and-tell, which Mongo briefly visualizes as a kind of puppet theater.

And the midgets march right past him, screaming away, eyes glazed, crazed by the repetition of words and the tramp-tramp of their own tiny feet, and disappear down the street, leaving him alone in unscreened sunshine on a bright Gomorrah day in the late Twentieth Century.

But Mongo's got the AA serenity prayer down cold, especially the part about recognizing all those horrors he can't do anything about—whole years, in Mongo's case. Life is better now, but he still doesn't go around deciding what's right and wrong when people do what they do. If midgets want to march around with Just Say No banners and faded pictures of claw-faced First Ladies—well, it's fine by him.

But midgets? Here he is, he's thinking, a man self-consciously putting a broken world back together, piece by shattered piece, and along comes something that belongs to another jigsaw puzzle entirely. After awhile the metaphor gets mean and instead of continuing toward Taco Time he turns off the sacred path and goes instead to his friend Klink's house.

Klink is home, smoking dope and watching CNN on a big screen. He works nights, as a janitor, cleaning up the schools. He motions Mongo in.

"Lookathere," says Klink, pointing to the TV. On the screen, Palestinian boys, caught throwing rocks, are getting their hands broken with rifle butts.

Mongo looks away. "Midgets," he says. "There's midgets running around town, having a Just Say No parade."

Klink turns to him, stoned-faced. "They weren't midgets," he says. He grabs his remote and mutes the TV. "They were third-graders," he says. "Part of the drug education in the schools program."

"They looked like midgets," says Mongo, but Klink has already turned back to the screen.

Klink's a news junkie. He knows what's happening. Besides watching CNN and the networks, he reads the *Gomorrah Informer*, *The Babylon Times*, *USA Today*, and subscribes to *Newsweek*. Several times now, he's written steamy letters to Connie Chung and Diane Sawyer and Mary Alice Williams, begging each of them to come to Gomorrah and live with him and be his love. Nobody's written back.

"This week," says Klink, "is all drug rallies in the schools. Classes have been cancelled. It's in the *Informer*."

"Third graders?" says Mongo.

"It's never too soon to say no," says Klink. "Huh," he says. "Lookathere." On the screen are tall white and black female models in orange fiberglass pods, the creations, from what Mongo can tell, of the Japanese clothes designer Elsa Klench is soundlessly interviewing.

"They looked a lot older than third graders," Mongo says, but it's useless. Klink's reality is safely contained by the margins of newspapers and the flickering colors of his TV screen. To the extent that Mongo's perceptions of the world as seen from a bike agree with what's inside those boundaries, Klink considers them valid. That's-the-way-it-is, is Klink's way of looking at it. Further investigation consumes time that could be better spent watching for late-breaking developments.

Anyway, Mongo's happy to concede that what he's seen is a bunch of third-graders being taught collective hysteria, and he's about to go when Klink switches to the Weather Channel. It's twenty minutes past the hour, time for the Five-Day Business Planner's Forecast. Klink watches it six, eight, ten times a day, looking for anomalies. He's convinced that Weather Channel announcers are being held prisoner in their studios and are trying to get coded messages to people on the outside. A hurricane where no hurricane should be, a drought in an area that once had plenty of water—these are cries for help.

Klink's talking about waiting outside some studio wall for his favorite Weatherperson, Jeaneatta Jones, to come slithering down a sheet, hop in his rented car, and come back to Gomorrah with him to live with him and be his love. "I'm going to save her," he's told Mongo, "from an entire lifetime of cold fronts, partly cloudy days, and average temperatures."

Klink thinks to offer Mongo his joint, but Mongo knows it's just a courtesy, and if he accepted, Klink wouldn't let him have it. All Mongo's friends are proud of him for getting clean of drugs. Offering the joint is Klink's way of telling Mongo he's an equal, that he can choose to refuse, and that Klink thinks he's strong enough to do it. If Mongo accepts, well, that's another matter.

Mongo watches all five days of the future and their crosshatchings of rain, sun, and thunder. When Klink switches back to CNN he gets up to leave.

"So soon?" says Klink.

"Gotta date," says Mongo. "I'll come back when you're not busy."

"Always busy," says Klink. "Lookathere." On the screen is a blonde woman in a silver leotard, looking like something out of a Nazi sex manual, selling a rowing machine. Klink bought one of the machines a year ago, and for awhile Mongo would come in to find him sitting in front of the TV and rowing away, sweating like a banshee—do banshees sweat? Mongo wonders—but it got dangerous. Klink was chopping up Ritalin and snorting it to get in the mood for exercise—he found lots of it at night, going through the lockers of hyperactive kids with his janitor's passkey—and toward the end he was spending a lot more time on the machine than he was sleeping. Also toward the end he told Mongo that it got easier once he figured out that the machine was rowing him. Now he's off Ritalin and also off the machine, smoking dope like a banshee, and starting to pick up a bit of a gut.

Mongo moves to the door. There were times, when Mongo himself was smoking dope, when they could talk.

"You gotta date?" says Klink, turning suddenly to look at him. "Who?"

"A counter person at Taco Time," says Mongo.

"The big one?" asks Klink.

Mongo starts to reply but by the time he comes up with a better adjective—she's not big, she's queenly, she's ample, she's goddess-sized, he's thinking—Klink has turned on the sound and is focused on the screen.

Back on his bike, burrito-bound once more, Mongo starts thinking about the parade again, thinking some of those third-graders did look awfully old, like they'd been working in a circus for forty years, or maybe had a bit part in the Wizard of Oz. He hates second-guessing his own perceptions, but he does it all the time. So he leaves the path to Taco Time a second time, and goes up the street where they disappeared, but they're gone, vanished, back inside solid schoolbrick or, for all Mongo knows, they've ducked inside the comfortable houses on this street, put on Raggedy-Ann and Andy costumes, and even now are leaning against nursery walls, arms and legs skewed, tongues lolling from their mouths, waiting for night.

By the time he gets to Taco Time she's gone. Lunch shift is over and the girls in brown uniforms behind the counter are hopelessly aged. Some of them are into their late twenties.

Mongo tries to think of what the thirty-seven year olds who went out with the high school girls of his youth would do in this situation, but he can really only remember one, who slowly drove around and around the high school in a beat-up '64 GTO, offering to buy beer for anyone under age. A loser, he knows now, someone, according to his alcohol-recovery literature, who was in that weirdly defined stage of alcoholism that finds the victim drinking with people he considers social inferiors.

So what are you doing here? he asks himself. He's sitting with a Tostada Delight and a Big Juan full of root beer and the big girl he came here to smile at and say hello to is probably in her afternoon psychology class, probably learning about guys like himself.

Mongo is aware that he's at the center of a pathetic tableau but he knows it's not his alcoholism that's at the root of it, it's his humanity. He's in the situation of a lot of thirty-seven-year-old men, trying to eliminate the last fifteen years, the ones with all the mistakes in them, and wanting to fall in love with someone innocent and pure and substantial and full of the knowledge that the world can be made whole. So why not? It seems like a more sacred impulse than Klink's obsession with anchor ladies.

But maybe not. After awhile he thinks of what he might do if he were really mature, if he were really looking to face up to the issues of adulthood, if he really wanted to restore the magic '64 GTO of his soul back to showroom condition. He stands up, dumps the debris from his tray into the little slot marked THANK YOU, walks out to his bike, and begins pedaling back toward house and home, toward adulthood, toward responsibility, toward—he'd almost forgotten—toward Kiki.

Kiki? Oh, God. And Mongo had been feeling so good. But now, on the big screen TV of his mind, a vision of a goddess fattened on a diet of rose petals loses color, fades, gets scrambled. He sighs. Kiki.

Flip back the pages of Mongo's life a couple of months, to the deep hard cold of winter, and find him in The Slaver's Rest one evening. It's nothing serious, he's just gone in for an O.J. or coffee. He's got friends there. Old friends. Just because a guy's suddenly given up alcohol doesn't mean he wants to stop sitting at a bar, talking about—he doesn't know, the Olympics or something. People at AA tell him it's risky business, that it's not the Alcohol, it's the Ism, but there are nights at home when it's just himself to fill up all the spaces in his house, and the spaces are way bigger than he is. He's afraid he'll get sucked into the walls. It feels safer—it really does, he thinks—to be cruising that part of town called Frustrated Desire, tipping the cocktail waitresses the difference between an O.J. and a screwdriver. They love him for it.

So sitting beside him at the bar is this sort-of-nice-looking girl, all alone—Mongo has a sixth sense about all aloneness, he thinks, and if he's wrong he can always say he's sorry when her boyfriend comes out of the restroom—and she's way thin. Mongo, joking, tells himself he isn't sure where she stops and her skeleton begins. And so, even though he's not really trying to prove you can be just as stupid after a year of being sober as you can after a week of LSD and tequila shooters, he says: "Annie!"

The girl looks up at him, slowly, like she hasn't got a whole lot of energy and to move quickly is going to burn out her last ten thousand brain cells. She says, "Who?"

"Annie Rexia," says Mongo, and just as it's out of his mouth he wants to climb under a table and rip out his stomach with a linoleum knife because he knows, under the heavy clothes she's wearing, that she weighs maybe eighty pounds and she really is anorexic, that what she's going through is analogous to his own addictions. He's just done the nutritional equivalent of calling her a drunk, a wetbrain, a non-functioning alcoholic—names people had called him once, names he had called himself, none of them helping the looks of his face in the mirror.

The girl looks at him and says no, her name is Kiki, but, yes, she does have an eating disorder and she's been in the hospital a couple of times for it and her doctor says if she goes in a third time it's going to be for an autopsy.

Mongo wants to die. And he keeps on wanting to die for an hour or two, because she comes to life and talks about it, about breaking an engagement and dropping out of Law School and her anxious mother and her angry father and her therapist that she no longer sees but who always looked at her with sad sad sad eyes. Mongo stays embarrassed the whole time, even after it's pretty clear she doesn't think he's a jerk. He's touched some deep horror in himself, just by sticking his foot in his mouth. Sounds anatomically impossible, but it's happened. He wants to make up for it. And somehow just looking her in the eyes has given him a case of the raging lonelies and he doesn't even want to think about going home by himself when he's feeling like this.

So after about eleven cups of coffee for him and a half-dozen Perriers and lime for her, he asks her how old she is and she says old enough and he asks her if she wants to walk him home because he's afraid of the dark. He says it like it's the truth—it usually is—and she says, with the devil-may-care air of someone who's going to the hospital a third and final time: "Yeah. Sure. You bet."

Once in his house, she wanders through the bare rooms, checking them out. She goes into his bathroom, and comes out without her bulky clothes, stripped down to a large men's T-shirt. On her it looks like a tent dress. Her knees bulge out from her legs. Her collarbones hold the shirt out from the rest of her body. She looks like one of those big-eyed children in a famine-relief poster.

"I like your house," she says. "Most people have way too much furniture."

With quiet self-possession she opens a hall closet, finds his sleeping bag hanging there, seizes its rustling bulk, drags it onto his dark living room floor and climbs into it. "Good night," she says. The phrase is alone, hermetic, complete. If hormones were galaxies, she'd be calling from Andromeda.

Two months later, and she hasn't left. She's not sleeping on Mongo's floor anymore, she's sleeping in his bed, but they lie there like children. No sex, even when he's asked. And she doesn't laugh at his jokes. And she's told him death is a place you can visit. It's nice there, she says.

On the plus side, she isn't expensive to feed, and—this is a first for Mongo—her mother likes him. And for someone who doesn't weigh any more than a medium-sized black lab, she fills a lot of emptiness.

Mongo, remembering all this as he rides homeward, gets embarrassed all over again, squints and shudders and starts pedaling like a banshee, begins to scream up the street, passing cars and scaring hell out of the people in the crosswalks. His lungs are hurting and there's a warmth in his head and thighs, and a shocky feeling that means in a minute or so his mind will dissolve into his body and he'll stop tormenting himself with tacky memories.

It happens. Suddenly all he can feel is sun on his back and the air cold in his teeth and the ecstatic agony of his own muscles. All he can smell is the sun-charged asphalt under his wheels. All he can hear is the hiss of wind past his ears. And all he can see is the dark curving hills that wall in the valley, black against luminous sky, marked pinto by the remnants of winter drifts. The street has shrunk to the width of the fog line, and he balances his wheels on it, pushing down, down, down, as fast as his legs will move.

Then, for a long time, no words in his head. A vague perception that he's gone past the city limits and is on the highway going north. On other days of other springs, he's ridden thirty miles this way, hypnotized by his own rhythm, balanced between thoughts. He has ridden until the dark and the cold of night have forced him to wake up, dismount, and flag down a pickup for a ride home.

But today, he wakes up too soon—he's only an hour or so out of town. There's a rise in the road ahead, a small one, but when he sees it he realizes he just can't just power up it like it wasn't there. Some momentary weakness of the spirit. And the flesh. Fifteen years ago, he believed the more you ran, drank, biked, loved, did pushups, did steroids, whatever—the closer to God you got. Gain was directly proportionate to pain. But no more.

Mongo drops the bike into a lower gear and slows down. All of a sudden he's in no hurry. Thirty-seven's too old to get on any Olympic teams anyway, he thinks, unless it's riding horses or Nintendo or something.

As he starts up the hill, it strikes him there must be half a dozen, or a hundred, or a million states of being. Two minutes ago he was the sum of sensation, and now he's pulled up and away from that and is looking down at himself, thinking: look, a middle-aged man on a bicycle. It's an image that worries him, and he begins to hope that things aren't what they seem, that he's different, that his body is the product of a unique genetic accident, so when he reaches forty his cells will cease their love affair with entropy, and begin the long and happy trip back to twenty, to strength, to passion, to wide-eyed innocence.

That being a remote possibility, he should maybe not give up on world-class competition. Maybe he should see these compulsive bike trips north of town as—what?—as preparation for the Tour de France.

It feels like a good idea, even if his body isn't the product of a unique genetic accident. Klink, getting fat smoking dope in front of his TV, looms as the alternative.

But then Mongo has the sudden, horrifying thought that maybe Klink's way is the right way. Klink goes to work, does his job, draws his pay, goes home, orders a pizza, turns on the TV and lights a joint. It's an existence that seems to have answered Klink's need for the sacred in life.

One day last summer, during a thunderstorm, a glowing, hissing ball came out of Klink's fireplace, bounced around the walls of his living room, and disappeared with a pop of implosion into a crack in the mantlepiece mirror. It left a mark that Klink says needed only to look a little more like Jesus Christ for him to be able to charge admission and make a fortune and have a CNN camera crew right in his living room. The Miracle Christ of Gomorrah.

Klink's enormous talent is to render the extraordinary into the commonplace.

It's a talent Mongo envies. A few winters ago, two weeks into a vicious and suicidal drunk, Mongo decided to throw himself on the upturned sword of malignant Divinity. He took his skis and sleeping bag and his abused body into the high mountains north of town, thinking that by camping out on some snow-covered peak where nobody would be looking, he would die of cold or hunger or UV exposure. It had seemed like a good idea at the time, the only chance he'd have of seeing God in his lifetime.

That night, while he sat upright in his sleeping bag, waiting bug-eyed for the end, shaking from hunger and cold and alcohol withdrawal, wonderful aliens began reach toward him from out of the centers of snow swirls. Real aliens. With big shimmering heads and deep shadowed eyes and spindly little silver bodies, held aloft by great wings. "Come with us," they whispered. "Come out beyond Saturn, beyond Neptune, beyond Pluto, out to where there's nothing but slow-drifting snow, and cold, and quiet."

It sounded fine. He would have gone with them, but for Klink's voice, which came out of a passing cloud: "They're just going to make you do stupid human tricks on the alien Letterman show." That sounded fine, too—better, at the time, than going back to Gomorrah—and he still would have gone with them except that Klink's voice had scared them away.

So he stayed awake and alive, waiting for more whispers. The moon rose up over the peaks, and lit up a landscape that looked to him just like shards of glass frozen upright in ice.

The sight moved him to address God. "Please, a sign," he said. "Give me a sign it isn't all meaningless."

Nothing. Even the stars hung still in moon-glow, not twink

ling. Mongo, for a long cold moment as still as the world around him, finally grew enraged and screamed out: "All right, Asshole, give me a sign it *is* all meaningless!"

There, far above the northern horizon, a star popped silently open, like an artillery shell too distant to be heard, and it spread broad bands of red and green light across the sky. Mongo slapped himself, pinched his arms, got out of his bag and did a little warm-up dance—but curtains of red and green continued to hang over the stars. It was fifteen minutes until they were completely gone.

So he packed his bag and walked off the peak—walked off it, afraid if he started skiing he'd fly off a cornice and disappear into deep space, and would, in cold dark vacuum, die a meaningless death. He made boot-shaped holes in the snow all the way down the ridge to the foothills, down the foothills to the flats, across the flats to his car. He drove home and warmed up in the shower.

The next day he walked over to Klink's house and told him what had happened. Klink told him his divine sign of meaningless-ness had only been a Russian satellite decaying out of orbit, spreading plutonium over half of Northern Canada. It was all over the networks. That night Mongo went to his first AA meeting.

So come back to the present. Look at Mongo from, say, the perspective of a god, or of the Goodyear Blimp. He's a tiny sunburn-colored figure on a great brown and white and green map-of-the-world, turning around on a grey line of road and starting back in the direction he came from. His bare knees and his spokes are flashing in bright white light. He looks pretty good from this distance. He doesn't look like he's suffering from the attentions of a malignant divinity, or if he is, it looks as if he's surviving, negotiating, and maybe finding for himself what is in suffering that's worth saving.

Mongo doesn't tell Klink much anymore. If he told him about the girl at Taco Time, Klink would know all about her, at least to the extent that she or her family or class at Gomorrah High had been in the local paper. Whatever mystery she contained would be explained by what Klink knew about high school girls, whatever voluptuousness she possessed would be covered over by Klink's "lookathere," and whatever Mongo and she might consummate would be delimited by what Klink knew about love.

He hasn't even told Klink about Kiki. How could he explain that he's got a strange, child-like woman in his bed who has all the sexy self-consciousness of a wild animal seeking warmth. He's already sleeping with a skeleton, and he doesn't want her reduced further, to the contents of a Sunday supplement article on eating disorders.

Still, Mongo needs Klink, because there are times when his drug-free perceptions get too scary for him, and Klink has to explain to Mongo what Mongo has just seen. Mongo has realized he never drank to make the world a stranger place or to do things he wouldn't do sober. He drank to make the world seem sober, to dim the grey steel monsters that he saw standing over human beings, pulling strings. He drank to whittle the thousand colors of the world down to a manageable seven. He drank so he wouldn't talk to winged aliens, and he drank so they wouldn't talk back.

A couple of years sober, and what's he doing? When he gets to Gomorrah he'll stop by the supermarket, talk the butcher out of five pounds of beef fat, and take it home with him. In the refrigerator, along with Kiki's hundred bottles of vitamins, homeopathic medicines, her tiny bunches of organically-grown vegetables, and her distilled water, is a big bottle of horse-capsules containing a natural fiber laxative. Kiki looks at her bones in the mirror and then goes and eats six or eight of them. Daily, they clean out whatever nutrients she's been able to force into her body over a tongue that does not taste, through a mouth that hates food.

Except that Mongo will—once again—go to the refrigerator and take the capsules into his bedroom, lock the door, remove the laxative from them and fill them with suet. He's calculated that Kiki's eaten twenty-one-and-a-half pounds of the stuff in five weeks. She's looking better, starting to gain a little weight—and she's frantically stuffing herself full of laxative capsules.

Someday, when she's up to normal weight, he'll tell her about his treachery, and as long as he's destroying her faith in him, he'll tell her that while he was lying awake beside her bones in the night, listening to her little-girl snores, he dreamed—when he wasn't dreaming of a girl young and round and in a Taco Time uniform—dreamed of making her, Kiki, whole, dreamed of freeing her from her metaphor of purity, dreamed of a life with her on the flesh-fouled Earth, and dreamed that she, in a sudden moment of grace, could turn and gaze at him with love.

A man stuffing big capsules full of beef grease for his love needs a friend like Klink.

Mongo, pedaling down the sloping highway, feels cold air streaming past him, feels the throb of hot blood under cold skin, feels his fingers go numb on his handlebars. It's six miles to town and the sun is down. In a cold half hour, he'll be at the butcher's counter. And after that, he'll wheel his bike into his garage and take a hot shower and come out feeling good, aware of every muscle he has. He'll look out over his town and see its thousand shimmering colors, hear its shrieks and sirens, and smell the decay of whatever hid in snowbanks all winter.

With no effort of memory at all he'll find himself walking the aisles of its supermarkets, sitting at the tables of its candlelit restaurants, lying drunk under a table in The Slaver's Rest, lying in bed with a half-dozen, twenty, a hundred big women who have given form to his own variety of starvation. And with no effort of imagination, he'll see Earth through Kiki's eyes, as a great overripe ball of food, and will try to find a way for her to face the terrifying rack of hunger.

He passes an intersection north of town. Cars are waiting there to get onto the highway. Mongo screams at their surprised drivers, leans back, pulling against his handlebars, screams loud and long, screams like a banshee, screams until a single thought brings scream to an abrupt end. Do banshees scream? he wonders. Of course they do. It's just that Mongo doesn't know if it's terror they're screaming, or want, or pain, or joy.

ENDORPHIN MADNESS

GODFREY IS RUNNING UP NORTH OF
Gomorrah on a cool summer morning. Somewhere below him is
the Lethe Creek Loop. His watch is counting the seconds from
when he crossed the bridge, started on the trail, and—after running half a mile—realized he'd done Lethe Creek six times in a
month.

So instead he's headed up the first ridge he's found with a path
on it, up toward the basalt cliffs of Gryphon Butte. Forty
minutes, he thinks. Forty minutes is what he'll allow himself to
get the soles of his Nikes above the mountaintop, and although he
knows better, he's got this fantasy going about it being flat up
there, with all the trees looking like they were drawn by
architects, the grass mowed, geysers and hot pools and little Greek
temples and undulating fields of flowers. And a race of beautiful
mountain nymphs hanging out there, eating grapes and waiting
for a guy like himself to come along and show them a fine time. If
he gets there in less than forty minutes they greet him with open
arms and he gets a hot date with the head nymph, all the peeled
grapes he can eat, and back rubs that don't stop at his back. But if
he takes forty minutes and one second or more, they toss him off
a cliff.

Godfrey's watch beeps off twenty minutes. He's running uphill
through broken rock. His trail has branched into rabbit runs,
coyote tracks, pika paths, attenuating all the way, getting fainter
and steeper, until he's finally facing plain hillside, rocks and scrub
juniper and Doug fir. It's as if there's a path everywhere he looks,
and for a moment he sees the whole world crosshatched with
possibility. Whoa, there, he thinks. Too heavy a thought for this
early in the day. Even skulls can get stress fractures.

Godfrey's got a trick he plays on himself when he's running

uphill. He tells himself he'll run a hundred steps and stop. When he does that he says no, it wasn't a hundred, it was a hundred and fifty. I can manage fifty more. When he counts fifty more he says to himself no, it wasn't a hundred and fifty, it was two-fifty. I can manage a hundred more because I've already done a hundred and fifty. So when he gets to two-fifty he promises he'll do a hundred before stopping. And so on, until he reaches a thousand steps run uphill.

But at a thousand steps, Godfrey doesn't stop. He's found if he staggers forward, his eyes blind with sweat and tears, his thighs and calves aflame, his lungs tossing up months-old phlegm, his mind overcome with pain and the need to stop, stiffen and die, he'll still gain some altitude. He'll get that much closer to the top and he's got to make it up there in less than forty minutes. Remember the mountain nymphs.

Sometimes it's not mountain nymphs. Sometimes Godfrey's running from small-town vigilantes, state police, CIA, creditors. If he makes this pass or that ridge he's safe from their helicopters, their lasers, their cluster bombs and their small-claims summonses. The odds are slim, but Godfrey's got the legs and knows the territory.

Other times he's the last free man in Idaho, running from a mob of zombies. Fundamentalist fanatics have taken over the government and they're forcing people into polyester suits and nuclear families. They've got this drug and it's way worse than heroin—they shoot you up with it and turn you loose and you run out and get married, enter an executive training program, lease an Audi, sign up for thirty years of house payments and start attending Lamaze classes.

Godfrey, counting 216-217-218, does a difficult thing, sighs between desperate gasps for air. These fantasies have a purpose, he knows. They drive him onward, upward, into physical agony— forty minutes, he's thinking, or it's flying without wings—so his body, hyperventilated, overheated, saturated with lactic acid and CO_2, covered with sweat, blood and dust, will release its internal morphines and get him higher than William Burroughs on a chairlift. Godfrey's an endorphin junkie.

He hasn't always been this way. Godfrey remembers back more years than he'd like to count, remembers being in The Slaver's Rest. He's at the bar, hunched over a beer. It's mid-afternoon. He's just had a couple of wisdom teeth twisted out of his jaw. The dentist's given him some Percodans. He's eaten a bunch of them, started on beer and schnapps and unfiltered Camels, and then all of a sudden the pain is gone and there are vague shapes out there in what had been the world.

"Aaargh-aarr-arrg-arr," says Godfrey.

He thinks he's saying, "Take 'em all out." If two teeth pulled feels this good, thirty or so more pulled will feel lots better. The bartender shape comes close and suddenly all Godfrey can see is what appear to be giant insect eyes peering into his own.

"You need some help, buddy," says the bartender, an old friend. Godfrey feels a coke vial pressed into his palm. He staggers by long habit to the men's room and shovels both nostrils full, using a McDonald's coffee stirrer he keeps in his shirt pocket. Sure enough, the the shapes out there start to shift and sharpen and they turn into semi-abstract walls and people, urinals, stalls, and about a million cigarette butts.

Godfrey checks out the mirror. Everything's fine, looks good, except for the pupils of his eyes, which seem to have been taken with a flash, and two holes he can see when he opens his mouth wide and tilts his head back. Voids. Voids, he giggles to himself, looking into them as if they were keyholes. How much surgery can a man stand? They could take it all out, he thinks, the muscles, guts, heart, bones, and blood, and you could still make a fortune in real estate. You could still make a killing in the stock market.

He tries to explain this, upon his return to the bar, to the woman who was sitting beside him, Suzanne or LaVicka or whatever it was—Annie, he remembers—and she finds the thought depressing enough that she gives him a half-dozen of her Prozacs. They won't take effect for a week or so, she says, but down they go and he feels better immediately. It's like the sun coming out. Somebody buys him a couple of shots of Jack Daniels and soon it's seven or eight and the sun's about to set, although you wouldn't know it in the darkness of The Rest or in the flickering torch-lit interior of Godfrey's skull.

Annie's got this idea that her life isn't going to be complete tonight without him. She wants to take him across the street and buy him a full cut of prime rib. Godfrey tells her sure, okay, he'll do it, even though the thought of a couple of pounds of bloodshot beef mixing with what's already in his stomach gives him an inarticulate queasy feeling. Whatever she has in mind, he tells himself. She's been telling him about her life and it sounds perfectly all right, something about divorce and getting screwed by lawyers, new beginnings, just wanting to take it one night at a time. Godfrey dips into his Percodan bottle, grabs the plastic capsule full of desiccant, the one labeled DO NOT EAT, and swallows it. What a rush.

Annie pulls him off his stool and the next person Godfrey sees is a hostess—Suzanne or LaVicka or somebody—he's not sure of her name but he thinks she went to Gomorrah High School with him, back in the sixties—asking them to wait thirty minutes and apologizing for the delay. She smiles when she recognizes him, says hello, takes a second look, pulls him aside, and says, "Godfrey, you look like you're about to die."

Godfrey grins at her, hitching the corners of his mouth on recently exposed molars. "Aaargh. Arr. Aagg. Aaaarrraaaggaa," he says.

The two women seem to be arguing. Godfrey nods genially and catches snatches of conversation:

"Can't you see the man is sick?" the hostess keeps asking. Annie is screaming he's taken, he's her date, leave them alone. Godfrey grins. This morning his world was all toothache. Now two women are fighting over him. How lucky it is he just happened in here.

Godfrey's still grinning when two people in uniform grab him and stuff him in an ambulance, grinning still when they whisk him into the emergency room of Gomorrah General.

"What seems to be the problem?" asks the doctor on duty.

Godfrey grins. "Aarr," he says.

The doctor reaches into Godfrey's shirt pocket and pulls out the McDonald's stirrer and what's left of the Percodans.

"Thought so," says the doctor.

Nobody wants to let Godfrey go home alone, even with a stomach recently pumped and a bloodstream full of narcotic antagonist. But he's managed to tell them he's uninsured, so they call the hostess at the restaurant—turns out her name really is LaVicka and she did go to high school with him—and she says she'll take care of him if they'll keep him until she gets off work. She shows up way after midnight. Godfrey's wide awake and hungry.

"Let's go to Nevada," he says to LaVicka. Something's missing in his life, and he's thinking maybe a slot machine could make him whole. "Free drinks. Free breakfast. Free money."

"We're going home," she says.

Once in her apartment, he checks out her refrigerator. He's horrified by what he finds. Carrots and celery. Fruit. Funny looking roots and sprouts. A spectral slab of prime rib flashes across his vision, and he has a quick sad feeling of deja vu, and loss.

"You got a steak I can fry up?" he asks her.

"I don't eat red meat," LaVicka says. "You shouldn't either."

He looks at her like she's crazy, but she launches into a lecture about nitrosamines, diethylstilbesterone, pyrogens, and cholesterol. Her job isn't being a hostess, Godfrey realizes. She's doing missionary work.

He gives up on food for the evening and tries to climb into her bed.

"You're too fat," she says, shaking her head huh-uh.

"Marry me," says Godfrey. "We'll change both your names."

She makes him sleep on the couch in the front room.

In the morning she's telling him, over bran muffins, that he's got to stop living like he's been living. "You're overweight," she says. "You're out of shape. You're doing too many drugs." She's been watching him from her station at the restaurant.

"Why can't you be like you were in high school?" asks LaVicka.

Godfrey looks at LaVicka's earnest face, flashes on the same face, chubby with teenage fat, staring out at him on the basketball court from a mass of Gomorrah High School pep club uniforms. Oh, God, he thinks. She's trying to fix up her past, and I'm in it.

LaVicka's lost weight. She's been telling him about her daytime job instructing aerobics. She seems to have found time to work on her tan. Godfrey looks her over. She coulda been a cheerleader, he realizes.

She wants him to stay with her until he gets his act together. Her apartment can be his halfway house. Nobody's made Godfrey an offer like this before and he's not sure he likes it. But he weighs forty-five pounds more than he did when he was playing high school basketball, and the women who have been trying to save him from himself seem to be having shorter and shorter attention spans. He sighs. It will be like waiting for death, he thinks. One way or another.

So over the next two weeks she's got him off pills, off booze, off cigarettes, off street drugs, and eating an olive-drab semi-solid that he thinks is spinach, aloe-vera, wheat germ, yogurt and fish oil all done up in a blender. He makes little kneeling statues out of it and leaves them on LaVicka's fireplace mantle. He tells her they're praying she'll bring home a doggie bag full of prime rib from work.

He doesn't miss the drugs. Enough chemicals are stored in his fat to last him years. As he loses weight, they leach into his blood. He's been getting high on hashish he smoked in 1967.

LaVicka has set up half a dozen jogging routes for him, one for every day of the week except Sunday when he's supposed to be in her aerobics class. She's made charts for his running times and weight losses and he's actually going along with it, shuffling up Moloch Gulch or out Neon Creek, eating the goo she serves him, staying out of the bars. He even attends the aerobics class, not for the exercise but because it allows him to become a socially camouflaged voyeur. He doesn't seem to be changing much but he's hoping that before long he's going to be lean and different and she'll stop grabbing his love handles and calling him fat boy. She still won't let him touch her and he's begun to want to.

He finally loses it, sneaks out to The Slaver's Rest to look for Annie and a night of skullpopping fun. He finds her but she's sipping a Perrier and telling everyone that her emotional problems were all caused by refined sugar. She spots him and wants him to go to an AA meeting with her. Depressed, Godfrey trudges back to LaVicka's apartment and her couch.

The next day, at the top of a nasty hill toward the end of a five-mile plod, Godfrey notices he's not in his body anymore. Hmmmn. He's floating twenty feet over his own head. His lungs are wheezing, his legs are hurting, he's got a side ache, he's sweating onto the pavement, he's getting stress fractures, ligament strains, hernias and blisters, but it's okay. In fact, it feels nice.

He sprints to LaVicka's apartment, pushing hard through smiling blue clouds.

"I'm cured," he says to LaVicka, and packs up his stuff.

"Stay," she says. "I'm getting tired of sleeping alone."

Godfrey realizes with a sudden start that it's happened, that he's begun his change back to her image of his youth. He can touch her now.

If he felt like it. But all he can think about is working out, eating pasta, getting in better and better and better shape. He's going to spend the rest of his life in sweat clothes. He'll keep a record of the beats of his heart. He'll pay a hundred and twenty-five dollars for running shoes.

"Good-bye," he says to LaVicka, and bounces down the steps of her apartment. He'll buy a Nautilus machine for his living room, that's what he'll do. Put it in front of the TV. LaVicka wails something behind the door he slammed, but he's got no more need for her.

So now, years later, Godfrey runs up the dark cliffs of Gryphon Butte. He's two-thirds of the way up and he's going to make it in time for a round of mountain nymph applause. He's drenched in sweat. His heart's on spin cycle.

He's once again crossed the frontier of his skin and thinks he's five stories tall. He's not just climbing hand-over-hand up the cliffs, he's bouncing, jumping, hopping up them. The rock is squeezable, friendly, organically grown. The sky has gone from blue to orange with little black dots all over it.

Over his shoulder, Godfrey glimpses a skewed and unearthly Gomorrah through sweat-blurred corneas. He gets a brand-new perception of the town as a great non-sentient colonial organism, its cells shopkeepers, waitresses, ski-bums, CEOs, Mafia hit men—everyone interdependent and more or less the same but shaped by caste-specific hormones at critical stages of growth.

What an insight, he thinks. Wow. It's what a drug-free lifestyle will do for you, he says to himself, and he likes the phrase so much he shouts it out to the rocks he's climbing:

"A DRUG-FREE LIFESTYLE," he yells, dancing past trees that have grown claws, on ground that has turned to quaking bog.

He's charging upward as fast as he can, but time is no longer a worry. He's forgotten about mountain nymphs.

He feels leaner and lighter with every step. His body fat was down to three percent last time he checked. He has a vision of himself in a few years, whittled to just a nervous system, a transparent brain surrounded by a whirlwind of spiderweb nerves, able to drift upward, electrically awake but motionless, on summer thermals.

He reaches the steep slope that leads to the rocks on top. He speeds up, lengthens his strides, and breathes with hoarse sucking gasps. He loses track of the number of steps he's taken. Arithmetic can't describe his world. Nor can any words prevail against the searing agony of legs and chest or the sound of the wind screaming past the raw ends of his Eustachian tubes. He sees colors, hears sounds, and moves convulsively upward.

And then he's on top. He falls to the rock below his feet. He gazes without comprehension at a twisted landscape of broken rock and wind-bent trees. He does not feel the sun warm his skin or hear his watch as it beeps at ten-minute intervals. Ladybugs crawl from beneath the top rocks and over his neck and he does not know their touch.

Over time, his heart slows. His skin dries. He wakes. A long time later language begins. "Rock," he says, and sees the world harden, crack, gather color, shape, and heft, watches colonies of lichen grow on it, sees it penetrated by the roots of trees and occupied by communes of ladybugs. He stands up, looks toward the west and sees the setting sun. Most of a day has disappeared from his life and he can't even remember it.

Godfrey walks slowly off the mountain, down toward Moloch Gulch, where Gomorrah is oozing up a golden pseudopod of big houses and vulgar foreign cars. He comes to a broad sandy hillside and begins trotting downhill and jumping an occasional sagebrush. Soon he's taking big leaps and running flat out over logs and bushes, swinging around the trunks of trees to control his speed. He knows why he's running—he's found a band of Nazis hiding out on the Butte. They're chasing him with flame-throwers and napalm. If he doesn't make it to the Moloch Gulch road in ten minutes they'll feed him to their German Shepherds as a hot evening meal.

He jumps down the mountain, fifteen feet at a leap, landing and falling, scrambling up and leaping again. He looks back and it's like he can see them, coming after him in smoking four-wheel-drive pickups with swastikas where their license plates should be. His heart begins to race, his legs begin to pump, and all across his nervous system little pusher cells start hanging around dark synapses, peddling pharmaceutical-grade endorphin.

But the trip down is over before he gets on another real jag. He reaches the Moloch Gulch road at a full sprint, sagebrush in his teeth, his running tights torn and his triathlon T-shirt contour-lined with dried salt, and immediately runs into what appear to be living, breathing mountain nymphs.

It's Suzanne and LaVicka and Annie, Spandex-coated and aerobicized and lean, running in a herd back to town to their health club. They're glad to see him and greet him with arm punches and bum slaps and questions about races he's going to enter. He runs with them to the club, where he showers and waits for them in the jacuzzi. Over the bubbling roar of the jets he hears them laughing and popping each other with towels in their locker room.

He relaxes, stretches out so the bubbles float him upward, closes his eyes to better feel the ache of his tendons and his bones, feels his muscles lose their cramps, and enjoys the fine end of a day just spent getting in even better condition. His neuroreceptors are quiet, satiated, riding easy, giving no hint that tomorrow they're going to be jangling for exercise, that they'll make every moment into an ache until he can get out on a steep trail and run his heart and lungs and legs and head to their limits.

When Annie comes out of the locker room, she finds him stretched out in the churning water, smiling, eyes closed, looking like a well-trimmed cut of beef. She reaches out and runs her hand along his thigh, feels the sharp definition of the muscles there, and runs her other hand down the hairs of his flat belly.

Godfrey doesn't feel a thing. He's lost somewhere in the perfectly reciprocating chemistry of his own flesh, adrift in a universe complete unto itself. It feels good in there and he's not going to come out. After a little more prodding, Annie gives up. Suzanne and LaVicka join her around the body, and while Godfrey floats in dreamless bliss, they talk about their lives and times and weights, and what they would like them all to be.

THERE'S A WRECK
AT THE TOP OF
MOUNT MAMMON

THE ANCIENT SKI PATROLMAN GETS

the male lead in a nightmare:

He's sitting alone in the patrol shack at the top of the mountain, when a voice comes over the radio and tells him he's late to a wreck. A bad one. In fact, a woman's skied into a lift tower and she's horribly injured. In fact, she's dead. In fact...but then the voice goes tinny and fades out before he gets the location.

"Where is she?" he asks the microphone. And he thinks, still dreaming, that he never likes the dead ones he hauls off the mountain. He hates the skull fractures and the coronaries and the broken necks. They don't happen often on Mammon, but they happen, and it seems he's always the one on the wreck. "Where is she?" he yells.

"Heaven," squawks the voice on the radio, and the Ancient Ski Patrolman thinks no, can't be, because Heaven's a big empty slope on the backside of the mountain, out-of-bounds and unpatrolled. She couldn't have run into a lift tower on Heaven because there's no lift on Heaven.

The radio is silent. He looks around the shack, looking for someone to help him, but he really is all alone. It must be everybody else's day off, he thinks, in dream-logic. And instead of calling for help on the radio, he walks outside, steps into his skis, and grabs the handles of a rescue toboggan.

And then, instantly and without effort, he's at the steep top of Heaven, sled trailing behind him, but Heaven isn't like he remembers it. It's got a new quad chairlift right up the middle of it and it's full of moguls and hundreds of people are skiing on it. And just below him is the body of a girl, lying in a trough between two moguls. He doesn't worry about the new lift and all the people

91

skiing out of bounds, he just eases the sled down to the body.

But the girl isn't dead, she's just lying there with her eyes open, breathing. No blood. He can't see anything wrong with her. When he asks her if she's hurt she just looks at him, mute. Head injury, he thinks. He needs to get her down fast. She doesn't resist when he places her in the long metal basket that's mounted on the sled, pulls the blankets and tarp over her and ropes her in. It's just a sled ride, he tells her. I've done it a thousand times.

But this time, when he grabs the sled handles and begins to ease her down—this time something new happens. The sled handles pull free of the sled. He feels them loose in his hands and looks back at the sled in time to see it sweep past him and down the slope, jumping over moguls, bouncing and tumbling toward a lift tower. He sees the girl struggling against the ropes, sees the horror in her eyes, sees her mouth wide in soundless scream. The sled bounces one last time and smashes into the tower. He sees the girl's upright silhouette against the metal, embracing it, giving it a last skull-shattering kiss. He realizes then that the dream itself has betrayed him, that it has used him to make itself come true.

Then he wakes.

□

The Ancient Ski Patrolman looks hard at his ceiling, trying to discern in its dim texture something more real than dream. Then waking more, he feels for Annie, his girlfriend. She moves away from his touch.

"No," she murmurs. She lies huddled away from him, her arms protecting her breasts. He leans toward her and kisses her in the center of her back. Then he turns to the bedside table, defuses the alarm, and swings his feet onto the cold floor.

Later, after a shower and a shave, he pours a cup of coffee for her and touches her again.

"Sleep," she says, and pulls the blankets over her head. He pours her coffee back in the pot.

He goes to his closet and pulls out long underwear and reaches to the top shelf for a fresh turtleneck. Seven of them are stacked there neatly, one for every day of the week. Over his years on the ski patrol he has grown to take satisfaction in seeing his long underwear and turtlenecks stacked in clean piles. He thinks it comes from always doing his wash at a laundromat. You can have bad dreams, he thinks, but they're never as bad as they are when you wake up to dirty laundry, too.

☐

The Ancient Ski Patrolman walks out of his condo toward the base of Mount Mammon. The dream is still with him. He walks the half-mile to the base lodge with bits of it drifting down through his mind. Dream-snow, he thinks. Covering the daylit world, drifting in between thoughts, making it cold back behind the eyes. And although the day is sunny, and it's March, he knows he will feel the dream's chill all day. And he'll volunteer to maintain snow fences or pick rocks on the bunny runs. Anything but run a wreck. He doesn't want to even get near a sled today.

He shakes his head, angry at himself. People don't lose rescue toboggans. He's never lost one. He's never worked with anyone who's lost one. There are stories, of course, of people screaming all the way to the bottom of the mountain when they looked out and nobody was at the handles, of baskets and their passengers that fell off the sled somewhere between the wreck and the ambulance, of patrolmen fired when they forgot to drape the chain brake over the front of the sled and it had run over them and through lift lines full of vacationing attorneys. But some of those stories he was sure were lies—he'd made them up himself—and the rest of them came from prehistory, from before even he came to be on the patrol.

Toboggans are stable, he thinks, even on the steepest slopes, even in icy conditions, even with large people in them. The girl in the dream—he sees her—is small and delicate and frightened of something, frightened into silence by a dream that has already declared her dead. But she's alive when he finds her. He tries to see her that way, tries to change the ending of the dream, tries to make his own mind less treacherous, but she still hits the tower.

☐

The Ancient Ski Patrolman walks into the base lodge and pours himself some coffee. Alfie, one of the younger patrolmen, motions at him, and he goes to Alfie's table and sits down.

"How's the knee?" he asks.

Alfie's bending over, adjusting his boots. He sits up and looks at his knees, one of which appears normal. The other looks as though his leg has grown a cantaloupe where his knee should be.

"The swelling is down a little, I think," says Alfie.

"You should go see a doctor."

Alfie shakes his head. "He'd just want to cut it open. All it needs is some rest."

That may be true, thinks the Ancient Ski Patrolman, but probably not. Anyway, it won't get rest as long as Alfie is working. Alfie manages to control himself most of any day, but then he'll get in the middle of a mogul patch and go shooting down through it, not feeling the pain, touching down on every third or fourth bump. It's what Alfie was doing when he injured the knee in the first place, tore the cartilage and probably a ligament. One of these days, something else in Alfie's knee is going pop like a rubber band and he'll get a sled ride to the ambulance.

"My wife wants me to quit the patrol, anyway," says Alfie. "Maybe I will. Maybe I'll get serious and do something with my life."

"Your wife would like that."

Alfie grins. "She would. She talks about it all the time. Says I'm refusing to grow up.

The Ancient Ski Patrolman laughs. "I wonder what she would say about me."

"She talks about you, too," says Alfie. Says it's too late for you to grow up. Says you missed last call. And she thinks it's people like you that cause people like me not to grow up.

And it was people like Alfie's wife, thinks the Ancient Ski Patrolman, who think that they can cause people like Alfie to suddenly want careers and stable relationships, children and good credit and respectable friends. Alfie will have all those things, and soon, but it won't be because his wife's a maturing influence. Instead, it will be because Alfie will have his knee X-rayed at the end of the season. And the orthopedist will indeed want to cut it open. Alfie will spend the summer on crutches, and when he remembers skiing every memory will have a little of the surgeon's knife in it. He'll know that all his flying came with a price. He won't be back on the patrol when the mountain opens next November. He'll have passed his real estate exam by then. He'll come up and stop by the patrol shack on weekends for a season or two. But the visits will get less frequent and there will be a time when Alfie will say to anyone who cares to listen: "I don't ski much anymore. I'm making up for lost time. I've got to put my kids through college."

When the knees go, thinks the Ancient Ski Patrolman, you grow up. He thinks back to a time in his life when he might have become a person with a couple of cars and a wife and a couple of kids and a house with a family room and an important job to pay for it all. But the injury has never come. His knees have held out. He hasn't broken legs or collarbones or dislocated a shoulder. And so he has shown up at the start of every ski season, ready to begin hauling wrecks down the mountain again. He is aware of a widening gulf between himself and those people with a material identity, almost to the point where he is of a separate species.

He has been married. It's something he remembers only indirectly these days, as though his marriage had been a long and tedious story about other people, badly translated from another language. He does know his wife tried hard to make sure he owned something. A few months into their marriage, she talked him into buying a condo not too different from the one he's living in. But she got away with it as her part of the divorce spoils. The condo never felt like home anyway, so he didn't feel much loss or the need to scrape together a down payment for another.

Home. That was where you went when the knees gave out. You ended up as a homeowner, horribly vulnerable to things like trees in pots in front of supermarkets, or table saws in basements. Or electric barbecues. Or toilet paper and lemon pepper in bulk. Sunday sale catalogs. It was no doubt a healthy development—the end, he supposed, of adolescence and the beginning of—what? He doesn't know. Post-adolescence, maybe.

☐

Annie doesn't push him to own anything, and the Ancient Ski Patrolman loves her for it. She seems happy enough with a roof over her head and food in her belly, and a bed to sleep in. This morning, he knows, she will sleep another couple of hours, then get up, eat something from the refrigerator, shower, and put on her ski suit. Then she'll make her way to the lift, flash her season pass at the ticket checker, and ski until the lifts close. She'll eat whatever he cooks for dinner and help him with the dishes. Then she will watch TV until it's time for bed. She will make love with him quickly, silently, and then turn away and go to sleep. She steals the covers most nights. She has, thinks the Ancient Ski Patrolman, an animal existence.

Even so, Annie's an animal he finds comforting to be near. She never bothers him about the future. She doesn't talk about her past. Abstract words like mortgage or maturity or commitment aren't in her vocabulary. She does pay her half of the rent and the groceries—divorce settlement, she explained the first time, handing him a check—and he loves her for that, too.

When she moved in with him, several people, Alfie among them, told him they worried about her intelligence.

"She's beautiful," Alfie said as they were riding up the lift one morning. "And she's got an incredible body. But she seems a little stupid. What do you talk about, anyway?"

"We don't talk," he told Alfie, annoyed not by the rudeness of the question but by the truth of his own answer. "And she's not stupid. She's just inarticulate. She doesn't spend a lot of time thinking about things. She just knows."

"Huh?"

"She's intuitive. She understands how things are without having to think or talk about them."

"Must be nice," Alfie said, and they rode the rest of the way to the top of the mountain in silence.

The conversation upset him. Annie's short sentences seemed adequate to her needs, and to his, while he was with her. It was as though her mind had come from an earlier time, when the language was just developing and was full of the concrete. Warm. Eat. Run. Sleep. She would say the words and he understood her perfectly. A world with no abstractions was a world tangible and secure. When she said love he knew exactly what she meant.

But Alfie's question began to haunt him, and he finally had asked her what she wanted from life, what she was going to do when she hit middle age.

"Never happen," she said.

"Tell me," he said. "Try to be serious for once."

She looked at him, surprised, as if the sharp grief in his voice was impossible to connect with the question. Then something flashed behind her eyes, like an animal running by a window at night. She said, gesturing at her body: "Before this goes, I'll marry someone again."

That was all she said, but she evoked a world with those words and told him that it was a world he couldn't enter. She told him that she understood him, that she knew he wouldn't or couldn't change, that she knew old age was kinder to the people who owned condos than to the people who rented them. It took care of any doubts he had about her intelligence.

□

The Ancient Ski Patrolman finds himself staring, with morbid fascination, at Alfie's knee. It's beginning to look like it has a life of its own. Alfie catches his gaze, looks down and says, "Cortisone. Maybe they can shoot it full of cortisone. Maybe they won't have to cut on it."

The Ancient Ski Patrolman gets up, suddenly tired of Alfie and his torn knee, suddenly not wanting to deal with sentences, short or otherwise, on his way to the top of the mountain. He walks outside, steps into his skis, skates to the lift and is on it before the attendant can get out of the lift shack.

He folds his shoulders and arms inward against the early

morning cold, leans forward and stares at the slope passing beneath him. It has snowed during the night, but a cold clear wind has come in after the storm, blowing what had been powder into hard little wind-packed drifts. Up near the top, the glazed tips of moguls will be sticking out of the new snow. Lots of wrecks today. Lots of snow that looks soft but isn't.

He wonders what Alfie's wife would say about his dream. That it is purely physiological, that it is merely the random firing of neurons into the night's empty sky? More likely she'd say it has nothing to do with growing up, getting serious, and making more money, and therefore isn't worth thinking about.

He thinks of the girl in the dream, then thinks that she's more than that, she's his own girl in his own dream. She's his own creation, constructed of materials stolen from the prison workshop of his skull. And she's mute, and compliant, and trusting, and it's his own fault that she gets slammed into his own lift tower.

He smiles, thinking of his irritation at Alfie, who knows better than to find out what's going on inside of his swollen knee. The image suddenly comes to him not of a cantaloupe, but of a small and conscious head growing in Alfie, a skull forming between femur and tibia, causing the swelling and the pain. The X-ray tech and the orthopedist are in for a grotesque surprise, and they'll explain it by hypothesizing an improperly absorbed Alfie-twin, suddenly growing again after twenty-five years of latent existence, using Alfie's knee-joint as a womb, beginning to dream. Alfie's going to be able to sell his story to a tabloid for a down payment on a condo. I ATE MY TWIN, the headline will read, AND MY TWIN ATE MY KNEE.

No wonder I have nightmares, thinks the Ancient Ski Patrolman, and then he knows that Alfie's refusal to find out what is going on inside of his knee is a healthy impulse. He wonders if Alfie has dreams, and if he does, if he tells his wife about them.

□

The Ancient Ski Patrolman is beginning to shiver. He thinks of

Annie, warm in his bed, head under the covers, making little muffled snores. He wonders what she thinks about when she rides up the lift. Nothing, maybe. Or maybe she just names the things she sees. Tree. Rock. Mogul. Cat-track. Ski patrolman.

There are better ways to embrace the world, he thinks, than to think about it. And he thinks that there was maybe a time when he didn't think about it so much, when he didn't dream of lost toboggans, before he had run a thousand wrecks to a thousand ambulances and before he knew more about knees and the things that could break in them than he cared to know.

And not just knees. He remembers his last time on Heaven. Three college kids had gone down it on the day after a storm had dropped eighteen inches of heavy snow. Two of them had showed up at the patrol hut that afternoon, telling a story, between sobs, of an avalanche and a friend somewhere under it. He remembers a cold sunset, and being in a long line of skiers side-stepping down through shifting snow, probing with metal poles, trying to hit flesh. And he remembers a small body, blue-faced and broken, lying in the glare of headlamps. He had run the sled that night, following the beam of his headlamp down through unfamiliar trees, moving slow and sad and deliberate, giving the body a more careful ride than he'd ever given a wreck that was still alive. He remembers thinking the absurd thought that if he hadn't been on the mountain that day, the avalanche might never have happened.

He thinks again of the dream and of the way it called to him so it could complete itself, and he thinks of Alfie and all the wounded young men like Alfie that are no longer on the patrol, and of the dreams that made them dance, made them fly higher and farther and yet higher until the human material broke and the dream had to fasten upon someone else.

He thinks of Annie, too, and wonders when her season will end and she will leave him to marry somebody else. He hopes she will stay long enough for him to learn to see the world without comment. He would like to tell her that, but there are no words in the language they share that would allow it.

☐

When he gets to the top of Mammon he looks back down the lift line. Empty chairs are coming up behind him, and he knows he has time to get one run in before everyone assembles in the patrol shack. He's cold, but he'll have time to warm up later. You never know how many more runs you have left in you, he thinks.

And so he skis back down under the lift towers. As the slope steepens, he feels his knees begin the thread their way down the mountain. His ski tips break through the wind-packed troughs between the moguls and then explode out over their tops, and he feels the unmistakable giddy presence of too much air under his feet. Then the shock of impact, and again, the breaking of crust, the explosion. He's flying. No wonder Alfie loses control every day.

He stops on the first cat-track and waves to Alfie and the others as they ride by above him. Then he pushes off down the mountain. I must not think about the end of this, he thinks, and that's the last thought he has until, a little later, he gets back on a ski-lift that on this morning, at least, looks as if it leads to the sun itself.

IDAHO MAN

AT AGE THIRTY-NINE, CHASE QUIT HIS
job as a professor of paleontology at the University of Babylon,
came back home to the little southern Idaho town of Ammoniah
Falls, and bought a run-down Texaco station. He's been there
since, running the station from a stool tilted against one of the
walls. Around the stool is a layer of beer cans and Bull Durham
wrappers, a layer beneath which his past has been carefully
buried.

But when he first came back he was asked to speak to the A. F. R.
—Ammoniah Falls Rotarians—about local geology. He gave a
lecture explaining why the landscape around the town is frozen
lava flows and cinders and dark river canyons that cut deep into
the South Idaho Plain. He showed them the fossilized vertebra of
a camel that had grazed locally four million years earlier. By
means of a time line that compressed the earth's whole history
into one year, he showed them that the moments of their lives
were inconsequential and few.

The Rotarians didn't care for the message. There were among
his audience fundamentalist Christians who regarded the piece of
camel as a lie invented by Satan. Others—the car dealers with new
models under wraps in their showrooms, or merchants with new
fashions in their shop windows—were upset by a vision of history
not marked by continuous happy progress. Because Chase, after
describing the cycles within cycles of earth's past, had ended by
describing the biggest cycle of all. Earth, he told them, would
someday be devoured by a fat and dying sun. Convertibles and
polyester suits and even the rocks upon which churches had been
built—all these would melt.

The rest of them were horrified by Chase's descriptions of lava fields red and flowing, poisonous gas drifting from cracks in the desert, and the thin green of river banks aflame.

It was only MacShane, the Ammoniah Falls mortician, who liked Chase's talk. MacShane was cheered by the perennial sequence of birth, life and death that gave his profession a dignity it lacked in the daylit world of Ammoniah Falls commerce. He looked at Chase's camel fragment and saw a vision of the earth as a vast graveyard, of dear departed creatures preserved in a huge sedimentary cemetery, all of them giving eloquent silent testimony to the embalming skill of God the Undertaker. MacShane asked Chase where he could get himself a fossil to show his kids. Chase gave him the camel vertebra.

"Fossils are everywhere," he told MacShane and the rest of the Rotarians. He smiled, as if this were wonderful news. Sullen businessmen studied their watches.

A week later MacShane came to the Texaco Station.

"I can't sleep," said the mortician. "I see it in my head, all ten billion years of it. You know how many things can die in ten billion years?"

Chase didn't answer. Morticians shouldn't have a fantasy life, he thought to himself.

"Since the human race began," said MacShane, "over seventy billion of us have passed over to the Great Beyond. That many dear departeds would require a cemetery half again as big as the West. Seventy billion top-of-the-line airtight aluminum caskets."

MacShane borrowed paleontology books from Chase. He gazed with wonder at illustrations of horn corals, trilobites, brontosauri, giant sloths, and wooly mammoths. He pronounced new names—Eocene, Mesozoic, Silurian—as if he were learning a language of love. If he spoke the name of an extinct species, it came out like a song.

"They all lived," said MacShane, holding one of Chase's books and pointing to a color plate of a large dinosaur munching on a small one. "And then they all—departed."

"Died," said Chase.

"Died," sang MacShane.

MacShane began drinking. Chase heard he had shown up at

several funerals drunk. A rival funeral home had begun to pick up some of the families who had been MacShane's steady customers. His wife was threatening to leave him. His children were demanding that he drop them off two blocks from Ammoniah Falls High School.

MacShane brought Chase a newspaper clipping detailing how the body of a miner buried in a South American copper mine had been discovered ten years later not as decaying flesh but as a statue of copper sulphate. The straining muscles of the man, the weave of his clothes, his hair, and even his dying grin had been replaced by blue crystal.

"He's a fossil," said MacShane.

"Technically, no," said Chase. "He's supposed to be 25,000 years old if he's going to be a fossil. But as long as nobody leaves him out in the rain, he'll last that long. Give him time. He'll be a fossil."

"Time," said MacShane, "there is plenty of. Give him his time. I declare him fossilized."

MacShane began to bring a jug with him on his visits to the station. He would sit in a chair he tilted against the wall beside Chase's stool. He would pass the jug to Chase and Chase would pass it back. When both of them were drunk, MacShane would curse time.

"You say the last eruption was two thousand years ago?" asked MacShane, pointing to one of the several black cinder cones that marked the city limits of Ammoniah Falls. "I piss on two thousand years."

MacShane had begun to see the world from the standpoint of its immense history. He claimed he could look at any man and see in him a long line of departed organisms all the way back to an original departed proto-DNA molecule.

"My wife," said MacShane. "She's de-evolving. Last week when I looked at her I saw a reptile. Today she's an amphibian."

MacShane's wife did leave him. She moved to Babylon with the kids and filed for divorce.

The next time MacShane came to the station he did not pull

up a chair beside Chase's stool. He stood in front of Chase, swaying back and forth, and stared down at him.

"I've found some fossils," he said.

Chase looked at MacShane with an immense weariness. His mind went back to a huge dusty warehouse at his university, one filled with cabinets which were filled with drawers which were filled with the hard dead bits of plants and animals.

MacShane began digging in his pockets. He finally found something and extended his hand toward Chase. In MacShane's palm were a half-dozen small white objects.

Human teeth.

"Fossils," said MacShane.

"Where did you get these?" Chase looked at MacShane. The man just stood there, emanating the odors of fresh alcohol and nervous sweat.

"If nobody leaves them out in the rain," said MacShane, "they should last practically forever."

Chase pointed. "Where did you get these?" he asked again. A crafty smile began flitting about MacShane's mouth like a small spastic fly.

"Oh, no," he said. "It's not that easy. I'm not going to tell you just because you asked me where I got these. It's just not that easy. You should know better."

MacShane nodded knowingly, turned, staggered to the door, swiveled his head around, gave Chase an unfocused glare, and left.

Chase watched MacShane weave down the sidewalk and lurch out of sight around a corner. He should have seen the signs before. MacShane, alienated from his fellow Rotarians by his dark profession, had finally reached escape velocity, had become twisted and wacko.

Chase felt a sudden guilt at having delivered the lecture at the Rotary meeting. He had supplied MacShane with that truth which subsumed all hope. The infinite geologic timescape, with its visions of island gardens rising out of the oceans and sinking again, of quiet forests being buried by volcanoes, of trillions of odd, discontinued animals hopping and jumping and slithering about—here was MacShane's defense against people who smelled death on him. MacShane could smell death back. If old age makes fools of us all, Chase thought, how much greater fools we are, viewed against the ages.

Chase shuddered. Morticians should not show up with human teeth.

But MacShane appeared the next day, sober, and apologized for leaving so abruptly.

"I've decided I want you to be my friend," said MacShane.

"Oboy," said Chase.

"I'm going to show you where I got the teeth," said MacShane, smiling. "Get in the hearse." MacShane pointed toward the black four-wheel-drive, smoke-windowed Subaru station wagon he used for unpaved departures.

The smile made Chase worry. If he takes me to the cemetery, he thought, I'm going to call the sheriff.

"I'm going to win a Nobel Prize for this," said MacShane.

"They don't give Nobel Prizes to fossil collectors," said Chase.

"I'm not a fossil collector," said MacShane. "I'm a paleontologist. Like you. Maybe you think you have to have a Ph.D. to be a paleontologist. All you have to have is a fossil."

"I'm not a paleontologist," said Chase, thinking of the tenured position he had resigned and its endless committee meetings and its burden of murderous university politics. And turf battles. Once a colleague had told him to stay out of the Cretaceous. "I sell gas," he said.

"Maybe when you see what I'm going to show you you'll want to quit selling gas. Hop in." MacShane giggled. "You don't even have to ride in the back."

He's going to kill me, thought Chase. He's going to take me out in the middle of the sagebrush and dump me in a collapsed lava bubble. Chase closed his eyes and saw, imprinted on his eyelids, an image of his own body, dead, crumpled, unembalmed, staring up at a sky rimmed by black rock. He felt a curious peace.

He got into the Subaru.

MacShane, whistling as he drove, took them past the cemetery and onto a dirt road which led out into the desert.

So if you're nuts and you're a paleontologist, Chase thought, you don't want another paleontologist around. If he finds the jaw bone you're searching for, he's the one who gets on the cover of *Time*. He's the one who gets to heft that bone and imagine what it must have been like to live on the other side of a million year-high wall. Could you murder a man for holding bones in his hand and inventing a whole world? And then Chase thought of an endless clear sky, under which small bands of laughing people gathered fruit from trees and snared small animals and sat close around fires night after night and sang and told stories. You could kill somebody for a ticket to that place, Chase thought.

Chase looked around for a weapon, spotted the heavy chromed club of a flashlight clipped to the underside of the dash in front of him. It made him feel a little better.

A few minutes later, MacShane drove up to the rim of a canyon. Like most of the canyons around Ammoniah Falls, its walls were vertical. The old lava flows had cracked into columns when they cooled, in a process analogous to mud cracking in a drying lake bed. When water cut through these columns, it toppled them and dissolved them away, leaving canyons that were narrow and deep, with pillared sides.

Chase watched as MacShane got out, pulled a shovel from the back of the Subaru, and walked to the edge. He wavered there for a moment, and Chase half expected him to turn and smile and then step off into short and blissful flight.

Instead, MacShane reached down at his feet and picked up a rope that had been tied to a large sagebrush growing out of the rimrock. "Come on," he said, turning toward Chase and gesturing with the shovel. Then he grasped the rope, stepped backward, and disappeared.

Chase stared for a few moments through the windshield, watching the sagebrush shake and bend with the tension on the rope. Then the bush snapped upright and the rope went slack. Chase got out and hurried to the edge, dropped to his knees, and peered over.

And looked down, down, down through four hundred feet of the thinnest, most transparent air, to where a short talus slope lay tumbled between the wall and the river. Junked cars, victims of final pilotless joyrides, lay crumpled and shattered and small amid great black stones. The ripples of the river were so far away it no longer looked wet. It looked like smooth green silk lining the bottom of the canyon.

MacShane was nowhere to be seen. Chase searched the rocks below for a broken doll-like body. Then MacShane's face and arm suddenly popped out of the wall thirty feet below him, where the far end of the rope fluttered in the wind.

MacShane waved something at him. A bone.

Even from where he was, Chase could see that it was a human femur.

He's discovered an Indian grave, thought Chase. He thinks he's found human fossils. He shook his head, smiling at his notion that he was about to be murdered.

But I could still die, thought Chase. He stared down at MacShane's disembodied head, its mouth open and moving.

Bones in a lava cave, thought Chase. He smiled at the irony of some poor Indian being dug up by a mortician. He wondered how MacShane would take the news he was only being an archaeologist, that, geologically speaking, he and the bones he was digging up lived at virtually the same moment in time.

But still, there was something—what was it? A memory, perhaps, in that femur, of people on a wide continent, living free lives, hunting pine nuts and seed, fishing for salmon, living under buffalo skin, moving when they felt like it. Land was free then. You could drink from the rivers. You could get old happily. People would make a place for you around the fire because you had learned where the hidden lines of force lay in the world.

Chase picked up the rope, tested the sagebrush it was tied to, turned away from the canyon and then stepped back into it. He felt a sudden giddy tickling on the bottoms of his feet as they moved out over more nothing than he had ever imagined existed.

It wasn't as bad as he had expected. By looking down as far as his feet and no further, he discovered cracks, holes in the wall, small ledges, all places where he could put a hand or foot. Of course, if the sagebrush pulled out of the rock above, he would die. Depart, as MacShane would say, on a four hundred foot journey, at the end of which he would join his gathered ancestors.

Then he stepped on a slanted ledge and a loose rock under his foot kicked out into the canyon and he was flying, slowed only by his burning palms as they wrapped hard around the rope. He yelled in pain and had half-thought a picture of rope-end when he felt himself swing forward a bit, into an empty space in the wall. His feet hit flat rock and his momentum slammed him forward to his knees.

Chase looked first at his rope-blistered hands and then around him. He had landed on a narrow ledge that protruded from a cave mouth. It wasn't a real lava cave, though, like the long caverns made when lava empties out from under a hardened crust. This cave had been formed when a river had deposited a thick bed of gravel and sand atop a lava flow. Then another flow had boiled away the river and locked its sediments in molten rock. In a later, cooler time, when the river had cut down through the lava again, the gravel had fallen out into the canyon. Where it had been was the cave he was in. Its roof was too low to make standing comfortable, but it was deep enough that shadows deepened to darkness at its back.

MacShane, apparently unimpressed by the suddenness of Chase's arrival, was on his hands and knees, digging furiously, scraping away the sand and rock from around a rib cage. The femur was beside him on the cave floor.

Chase picked it up. It was heavy. It was not bone. It was opalized quartz shaped like a human bone. It was old. Far older, he thought, than any Indian. It was one thing for replacement to go on in a highly mineralizing environment, as in a copper mine. It was another for enough silica to leach out of the basalt to turn bones into opal.

He hefted the femur, and watched its pale iridescence against the black cave walls. That iridescence came from tiny spherical droplets of quartz, formed in wet darkness over years so many as to make a human life into a quick snap of divine fingers. And during those years, as far as any paleontologist knew, humans had not walked the earth. This bone—this thing—should not exist, he thought.

He wondered about the original owner of the bone, who must have used it to walk over a land alive with herds of horses and camels and elephants. Did he walk hand in hand with another of his kind? Did he point at the spring-dancing animals? What words did he say to the sun in the morning? Thank you, Chase thought. It's what I would have said.

He saw then, in that cave, a gateway. All you had to do was find the right shadow in the back, step into it, and people would be there, people with two million or more years of bright future ahead of them, living where the weather was gentle, the trees laden with fruit, the rivers full of fish. And they'd greet you with open arms.

"Look at this," said MacShane. He held an object between his hands as though it were a chalice. It was a skull. Like the femur, it had been opalized. Sand, in small hard chunks, trickled out of its eye sockets. It was human. The cranium was large, Chase thought, as large as any of those tottering along the streets of Babylon atop more modern spinal columns. The jaws and remaining teeth—the ones not in MacShane's pockets—were small, delicate, only a little predatory. He wondered what kind of mind had been matched with them. Maybe one that could live for a hundred thousand generations without betraying the earth with its presence. Chase gently took the skull from MacShane's outstretched hands.

"You're going to be famous," said MacShane to the skull. "You're going to be Idaho Man."

Looking up from the skull's eye sockets into MacShane's eyes, Chase had a sudden sympathy for the man. The bones MacShane had found, the beautiful bits of a creature unknowable and long dead, had seduced MacShane irrevocably. Never again would he be able to see time measured by anything less than lifetimes.

But by staring into the eye sockets of the skull, Chase thought, MacShane might also have seen a gateway—to where he didn't know, but he had an idea it was to some sanctuary, eons away, where you didn't have to embalm bodies and smile for a living.

Then Chase thought of the people who would flock to a discovery of this importance, the experts and theoreticians and paleontological prima donnas, and finally, the philosophers who would come forward to speak as members of a newly ancient species. MacShane's fossils would be taken from him. His bones would be given to those who could say what his bones meant.

Chase thought of the quiet town of Ammoniah Falls, and of his own recent return to it, and of being a paleontologist who returned to a place where fossils didn't mean much, where no one much cared about whether a rock had once been alive or not.

"What will you say to them?" he asked MacShane. "What will you do when they pull you back from that sanctuary, back into the here and now?"

MacShane didn't know what he was talking about. But he turned away from Chase and looked across at the far canyon wall.

"You can see all the layers over there," MacShane said, pointing. "Lava flows on top of lava flows. And they're all on top of a sea bed. The earth is old, Chase," he said, and these words, too, sounded like a song.

"I know," said Chase. And then he took a step back into the cave, placed his foot on the small of MacShane's back, and pushed with all his strength. MacShane shot forward, into open air. His arms and legs waved for a second, reaching for something solid. Chase heard him hit the talus a few seconds later.

Chase placed the skull and femur gently, almost reverently, in the center of the bones MacShane had been excavating. Then he began the delicate task of burying them again, shoveling fine, drifted-in cave dust around them until they were well-covered, then covering them with coarser gravel and slabs of lava. When he was done, there was only a steep slope of rock against one side of the cave, with no indication that anything lay under it.

He ran the shovel through his belt and with burning and weeping hands grasped the rope. He climbed slowly back up to the canyon rim. This time he made no mistakes, and when he reached the sagebrush he untied the rope and coiled it. He looped the coils over his shoulder, picked up the shovel, and began the long trek back into Lost River, staying off the road so his tracks wouldn't be noticed. Halfway there he tossed shovel and rope into a lava tube. They rattled down into the earth for a few moments. Then there was silence.

MacShane was found a week later, after an air search discovered his car. He was declared a suicide. No one thought to examine the canyon wall thirty feet below his parking spot, because no one thought MacShane would climb down thirty feet to ensure a softer landing. Successful suicides are given credit for common sense.

Chase remains at the Texaco station, pumping gas for an occasional car, cleaning the bugs off an occasional windshield, but mostly sitting on the stool against the wall and contributing to the sediment around it.

He has not been back to the cave. There is plenty of time for that, he thinks. Plenty of time to call in teams of bright young paleoanthropologists eager to become famous. Plenty of time to scour the floor of a cave for pieces of stone that could change what it means to be human, here and now in Ammoniah Falls. And best of all, he thinks, there is plenty of time to sing in dreams with all the dead who drift beneath the South Idaho Plain, one of whom was named MacShane.

M. I. A.

JUNE. THE SKI RUNS ABOVE GOMORRAH are green with new grass. Half-grown leaves hide the skeletons of cottonwoods. Motorhomes migrate north to thawed campgrounds. Gallery workers put up fresh Western Art.

It's a sunlit evening. Renwick is tending a backstreet bar. His customers are golfing, kayaking, windsurfing, or selling real estate. He's alone, reading a brochure he found in the Post Office trash can this morning. It announces the reopening of an old dude ranch in the mountains forty miles north. He pauses over pictures of peaks rising behind a rustic lodge, horses, cabins, and sunbathers beside log-enclosed pools of natural hot water.

He checks prices, tosses the brochure down the bar, and is pulling himself a beer when—UH-OH. SOMETHING'S HAPPENING.

The sunset sweeps into the room in a lurid vortex. Ecstatic voices come from the jukebox. The waterfall in the beer sign above him fills the back bar with tinkling crystals of ice. The floor breaks into shards, and he's falling down dowowowowowowowo—.

Okay. No need to worry. Just a flashback. Friends of friends have staying at his apartment, peddling acid, turning him on to the good old days, before angel dust, before Altamont, before Dylan got religion. So enjoy.

Anyway—this is sooo real—he's fallen into a hot pool at a dude ranch—he's sure it's a dude ranch—holding—who? Hey, it's Annie— in his arms. Stars pinwheel overhead. Moonlit fog drifts over the water. Annie sits between his knees, her head on his chest. He slides his hands over her ribs until they cup her breasts. She turns, takes his head in her hands, kisses him, and pulls him to her. As they float over deeper water, she crosses her ankles behind his back and draws him down to the bottom. Breathing is no problem.

117

Beer, overflowing his glass, pours over his hand, flows down his arm to his elbow, and drips on his shoes. He fights back to the surface of dream. Where'd that come from? he wonders. What's Annie doing in a flashback of mine?

Annie's the new waitress. Renwick's asked her out four times. She keeps saying she's busy, and finally Renwick has decided that women, like heartbeats, are many but finite. Time wasted on Annie could be better spent on the sad divorcees—the white wine trade—who come in near closing time, and who respond with inappropriate gratitude when the bartender comps them a Chablis.

Renwick picks up the brochure again. He's been meaning to fix up the apartment. It can wait. He calls Annie.

She answers on the first ring. "Renwick," says Renwick. "What do you say to a hot weekend at a dude ranch?" He reads her the pitch from the brochure.

Silence. Renwick's thinking she's quietly hung up while he's been talking when she says, "Why not?"

Renwick grins. It wasn't a flashback, he thinks. It was a vision of the Holy Grail.

Saturday morning he's putting her bag in his car. "This will be fun," he tells her.

Annie smiles at him. "Nice car," she says.

It's Renwick's Porsche 928. Renwick's bought it over the phone from a Babylon insurance company. It's urban decay on wheels, having been in one of the Babylon riots of the last few summers. It's got bullet holes. The passenger window is poly sheeting and duct tape. The windshield is spiderwebbed. Because it didn't run, Renwick's taken it to a friend who deals in car parts. After weeks of cutting and welding, they've shoehorned a Plymouth slant six under the hood.

It doesn't go as fast as it once did. The fenders are weld-burnt. The shifter is hose-clamped to the steering column. But the seats are leather and the stereo still works. Renwick cruises Gomorrah in it, running his window up and down and sneering at the drivers of lesser Porsches.

Renwick and Annie leave Gomorrah and drive north. Renwick

predicts lakes and rock formations. Annie points out unicorns in clouds.

So what, thinks Renwick, if the first four times I asked her out she laughed. She obviously can appreciate me now.

At a high summit, he pulls off at an overlook. They gaze out on twenty miles of high peaks, white above dark lodgepole foothills. The meadowed valley below the lodgepole glows with water-mirrored sunlight.

"Oh, it's beautiful," Annie says. "Oh."

"You've never been here before?" asks Renwick.

Annie says she's mostly lived in California. Renwick wants to ask about college, marriages, children, and if she's wishing she was with somebody else, but he's afraid of wrong answers, stories of love and grief. He names peaks.

Down along the river, they drive by sandhill cranes strutting on the banks. Wildflowers color meadows yellow and blue and Annie, who's brought a camera, makes Renwick stop so she can take pictures. She wants to take one of Renwick.

"Huh-uh," Renwick tells her, pushing his palm at her. "No pictures." An old girlfriend, Suzanne, has been sending him photos that she's taken of him years ago, backdropped by these same mountains. She's drawn on them—knives in his heart, nooses around his neck, steel traps clamped over his crotch. He knows what he didn't know when he was living with her. She liked him.

"Come on," Annie says. "It's not going to steal your soul."

But Renwick doesn't know that for sure. He's relieved—a dozen miles later—when he sees the turnoff to the ranch.

As Renwick and Annie drive through the ranch's gate, they see helicopters parked on the lawn in front of the lodge.

"Friends of yours?" asks Annie, pointing.

"People I know," he says.

It's not quite a lie. Since reading the brochure, Renwick's done research. The ranch is owned by a syndicate of Gomorrah businessmen, some of whom drink in his bar and talk endlessly about the Sixties, when napalm and California subdivisions were moving as fast as they could make them. They bought the ranch as a private club, but benign features of tax law led them to open it to paying guests.

Renwick checks in at the front desk. A young cowboy points to their cabin.

"Nice car," says the cowboy, looking outside. "Even if it is beat-up."

"Runs like a thoroughbred," says Renwick.

At the cabin, he carries their bags inside. Annie takes her bag into the bathroom and comes out wearing jeans and a cowgirl shirt. She sits on the bed, pulls on spike-heeled cowboy boots, and tucks her jeans into them.

"Long hot trail," Annie says. "Let's go get a drink."

On the way to the lodge, Renwick links his arm through hers. Walking up the lodge steps, he catches a whiff of sulfur from the pools. Coming here was a good idea. With less awareness of the possibilities of life, he would have just asked her to a movie again.

But they don't have time for a drink. Dinner is being served in the crowded dining room that adjoins the bar. A waiter, the same cowboy who checked him in, leads them to a small table where two other people are sitting.

Annie is seated by a thickset cowboy who introduces himself as Cash. Renwick's seen him once or twice in the bar, in business clothes, and thinks he may be a Gomorrah local. Some people in town have real jobs in Babylon, and Lear jets to fly them to and from work. Cash peers at him. "Whose cabin you staying in?"

"Ours," says Renwick. "We came up for the weekend."

"Oh," says Cash. "Guests." After a short silence, he says, "I own this place."

Annie smiles at Cash. "Your helicopters?" she asks.

Cash scowls as pounds of prime rib are dropped on his plate. The waiter is wheeling around a tiny chuckwagon. "I have partners. They're noisy with their wealth."

"We came up in Cash's Ferrari," says a soft voice. "It's less noisy." Renwick turns to the person sitting beside him, a voluptu-ous—girl, thinks Renwick. She's wearing a denim skirt and check-ered blouse. A cowboy hat rests against her shoulder blades. Platinum-blonde hair feathers back from a face that still holds a baby-like softness. The rest of her, Renwick notes, is fully adult.

"Weena," says Cash, pointing her out with his fork. "She's with me."

"I love Ferraris," says Annie.

"Renwick," says Renwick, pointing his fork at his jugular. "Annie," he says, pointing the fork at Annie's ear.

"A pleasure," says Weena. She sticks a plump hand at Renwick. He shakes it. Weena and Annie smile at each other. The waiter moves to Weena's plate.

"Not too much, " says Cash.

The waiter puts a tiny slice of meat on Weena's plate, gives Renwick and Annie more than they can eat, and goes to another table.

Cash begins talking about a company he owns, which manufactures fertilizers and industrial chemicals. From small beginnings in Babylon, it has expanded to all the way to equatorial countries.

"It's ironic, isn't it," says Cash, "that the same material can be used to make life—and death?" He explains that some of the compounds his firm manufactures are used to make both fertilizers and munitions.

Renwick pokes at the meat with a horn-handled steak knife. Blood is all over his plate.

"Buffalo," says Cash. "I got a herd on a spread up in Montana."

"Mmmmmm," says Annie.

Renwick turns to Weena beside him. She's sneaking food from his plate to hers. She giggles.

"Don't tell," she says.

Renwick looks to see if Annie's watching, but she's looking at Cash. Renwick looks over Annie's shoulder at the waiter. He's against the wall under a moose head, looking at Annie.

Annie. She has big grey eyes. They're gazing in wide admiration at Cash.

Irritated, Renwick shifts his gaze to her nose. It's perfect. He wants to touch it. The waiter seems to be looking at her nose, too. Renwick looks at his plate. Weena has stolen half his prime rib.

Then a shadow slips between Renwick and the table. He's standing alone on a dusty windswept mountain, watching, in the clouds above his head, a dude ranch of the mind. In its lodge, a banquet: the stars of Western movies at ambrosia-laden tables. He hears laughter and has a notion of a species better than his own shabby and short-lived one.

Gripping the table in front of him, he looks around at men in boots and shiny shirts, and at women in dresses he's only seen in sepia-toned photos, and back at Cash and Annie. He wishes the little polo player on his shirt could be magically transformed into a bull rider.

Cash turns to him. "Howyadoin?" he says.

"Okay," says Renwick. "Okay."

"Good," says Cash, with a host's grin. "Good." He turns and says something to Annie. Renwick inspects his plate. Weena's dug a hole in his potatoes. A side dish of carrots is gone.

"Fascinating," says Annie.

Renwick realizes he's alone. He tries to stop his thoughts, but when he looks at Annie she seems impossibly distant. If he could only touch her—but she's been picked up by the wind.

He again looks at his plate. It's empty.

Dessert is served, a chocolate mousse the waiter calls an elk. The moose in the area, he explains, were killed off years ago. Weena doesn't get any. Renwick eats his quickly.

"Tell you what," Cash is saying to Annie, "I'll borrow a chopper tomorrow and give you a ride. Borrow a pilot, too. Never did learn to fly one of them things."

"Hear that?" Annie asks Renwick. "Helicopter ride." She kisses Cash on the cheek. "You're a dear." She looks at Renwick and smiles. "Fun," she says.

Cash looks at Renwick. "We'll give the boyfriend a ride, too."

"He's not my boyfriend," says Annie. She laughs. "I mean, we haven't known each other long. Just—."

"I understand," says Cash. "There's a man here tonight I'd like you to meet. He's a pilot, but he's no civilian. "He's a hero. A P.O.W. Been in Laos for thirty years."

Renwick keeps his bar's patrons on a steady diet of CNN, figuring they'll tip more if they know the world he's offering refuge from. Shot-down Vietnam war pilots are rumored to have been waving at people in Thailand from across the Mekong. Renwick's seen angry relatives and embarrassed State Department spokesmen, but he didn't know the pilots were home.

"He's here in this room," says Cash.

Cash points to a man in a chair against a far wall. He's gaunt and grey, and his civilian shirt and pants hang on him. Old sizes too large, thinks Renwick. He's shrunk. The man stares at him with bright, unfocused eyes.

"They shot him down on one of the first sorties we flew," says Cash. "He parachuted into a village. They put him in a cage for thirty years."

"That's terrible," says Annie.

"Worse," says Cash. "Let me tell you something else. Those people are savages. If it wasn't for this country they'd still be barefoot, praying to rocks."

"They worshipped rocks?" asks Annie.

"Worse," said Cash. "They're Buddhists." He pauses, studying Annie. "That boy over there has been through hell," he says. "Nothing's too good for that boy."

Renwick closes his eyes and—and he's flying low, releasing napalm canisters. Blooms of flame below. Then—whoops—flame in the cockpit with him, the violence of ejection, the brief peace of the parachute. Then the people who gather around, each of them holding a rock. One of them speaks. "You," he says in Laotian, "have fucked up."

"While he was in that cage," says Cash, "I was here in America, running my business. Look at this." Cash waves at the log walls and beyond, out an open window, to where a beautiful woman in a long gingham dress sits on the helicopter-shadowed lawn, her arms around two children.

"We take this for granted," says Cash. "That boy over there don't take it for granted." Renwick looks at the boy, who looks bird like and ready for a rest home, and then looks at the woman on the lawn. The Madonna of the Helicopters. Somebody takes that woman for granted. Renwick, feeling something like kinship, looks again to the pilot.

Cash turns to him. "What'd you during the war, anyway?"

"Threw bricks at cops," says Renwick.

Cash gives Renwick a nasty smile, and says, "I hired a band."

"Huh?"

"I hired a band for that man. To let him know he's home and folks care about him." Cash stands up, turns on the heel of his cowboy boot and leaves the room.

Renwick looks at Weena, expecting her to go with Cash, but she sits and watches Annie's dessert with pure longing.

"Is Cash always like that?" Renwick asks her.

"Rude?" asks Weena. "Yeah. Always. You get used to it."

"Didn't think he was rude," says Annie. "Thought he was nice."

"You do get used to it," repeats Weena. "You'll get the chance."

Annie ignores her. "The pilot," she says. "Don't you feel bad?"

Renwick shrugs. He doesn't. "Now that dinner's over," he asks Annie, "You want to go soak in a hot pool?"

"Very sad," says Annie, standing. "Let's dance."

She walks away from him, out of the room. Renwick follows her to the ballroom of the lodge, and walks to her and puts his arm around her waist. She moves away from him, and looks at him in a way that has nothing in it to show she has ever known him.

The band sings about cold winters, warm women, and cozy cabins under pine trees. Couples run out on the dance floor, flailing their arms and jumping up and down.

Then Annie appears to see him. She tugs at his arm. Renwick shakes his head and shouts that he doesn't know how to dance this way.

The waiter crosses to them and wordlessly pulls Annie out onto the dance floor. At first she looks like an expert dancer but Renwick notices it's passivity and not grace that moves her. She smiles and relaxes, and the waiter pulls and twirls her about. Renwick closes his eyes and sees, embossed on his eyelids, the schematics for a state-of-the-art Japanese android, complete with patent leather skin, nitinol muscles, hydraulic sphincters, a PVC skeleton, her single glittering microchip programmable for all night dancing, singing, if need be—.

When the band pauses, Annie is delivered to Cash. She's spun and twisted all over again. Cash's face, red and sweating, bobs in front of Renwick. Renwick thinks heart attack, and finds the thought pleasant.

He decides to leave and find some quiet place and, if imagination can point the way, go back to that time before dinner, before Ferraris, helicopters, music, and the shot-down pilot.

He looks through the crowd for familiar faces and spots Weena stretched on a couch in the corner of the room, looking at him. She yawns and appears to sleep. Beside her, his hand gripping the arm of the couch as if it's the control stick of a plane in a dive, is the pilot.

The music stops. Cash escorts Annie to the couch, stops her in front of it, and gestures that the pilot is to dance with her.

"Annie!" screams Renwick. Too late. A steel guitar drowns his voice.

Renwick watches the pilot as he embraces Annie and rotates to a beat not coming from the bandstand. Annie gazes, serene and sleepy-eyed, over the pilot's shoulder.

Renwick hurries out of the room and finds himself on a balcony above the lawn. Moonlight. Cool air. The helicopters shine above dark grass.

There is movement beside him. A hand touches the back of his neck.

"Don't just talk to yourself," says Weena.

Renwick jumps.

"It's hard to make friends if you're shy," she says.

She moves closer. "Thanks for keeping me from starving."

Renwick stares at her moonlit form. She's all curves. In more reverent times she would have been paraded through spring fields to make corn grow.

She moves forward and he moves back until he's against the balcony rail.

"You're not having fun," she says. "I felt sorry for you at dinner."

Renwick turns away. "Don't."

"Your loss," she says. Her breasts push against him.

"Your Annie seems to be quite popular," she says.

He tries to move away but the rail stops him. "She's not my Annie," he says. "Didn't you hear her?"

Weena laughs. "Bet you had big plans for the weekend, huh?"

"We're just friends."

Weena sighs. "Like Cash and me," she says.

He's trying to think of something to say to make her go away when she grabs his head and kisses him on the mouth. Her tongue pries between his teeth. He pulls away but she puts an arm across his back and holds him close. He feels the swell of her abdomen against his, the pressure of her breasts, the—UH-OH. He's getting a hard-on.

She releases him and steps back. "Do you suppose anyone saw us?" she asks.

Renwick knows what Cash will do to him. He sees himself, bound and gagged, being tossed from a helicopter a mile above the lodge.

"Below the kitchen," says Weena. "is a cellar. There are whole freezers full of ice cream. Meet me there."

"I'm not going to meet you anywhere," Renwick says.

"Might as well," says Weena. "You won't see Annie again tonight."

"What?"

She smiles sweetly, her baby face innocent of lies. "She seems to have a thing for Ferraris and helicopters," she says. "I'll see you in the cellar."

"Forget it," says Renwick.

She walks away and looks into the room. "Your Annie's dancing with the pilot. Scary. He's not all there." She blows him a kiss and disappears.

Renwick leans on the railing and stares at the lawn below. So he made a mistake. At least he doesn't have to watch it enacted. He's going to tell Annie he'll be out in his car, trying to pick up a ball game on the Blaupunkt.

If she gets tired of dancing she can come knock on his window.

126

If she says she wants to go soak in a pool, lean up against him, make wavy patterns in his chest hair with her fingernails—he'll think about it.

But when Renwick walks into the lodge, he can't find her. He makes his way around the dance floor but—no Annie.

Wait a minute. The waiter. Renwick remembers his fascination with Annie's nose. He's probably kissing it right now.

But when Renwick runs into the dining room he finds the waiter at a table talking to the Madonna of the Helicopters. They are alone in the room. The waiter catches Renwick's eye, grins, and puts a finger to his lips.

Renwick backs out of the room and runs down the steps of the lodge. He supposes Annie got upset when Cash forced her to dance with the pilot. Or maybe—OH, NO—she came to look for him on the balcony and had seen Weena with her tongue in his mouth.

That's it. Suddenly he knows what Annie's feeling—she's back in the cabin, staring at the logs, terrified, lonely, having been driven into the wilderness by this person, this Renwick, who seemed sexually acceptable—until he left her alone at the dance. She's wondering if she'll ever get a ride back to Gomorrah, because Renwick's gone off with someone else, with that awful girl, she saw him there, on the balcony—. Renwick pushes open the cabin door.

Annie's not there. In the bathroom he finds her bag, her traveling clothes folded over it, on the floor.

Then: Oh, God. OH, GOD. The pilot. Renwick's mind releases old psychiatric headlines. Delayed stress syndrome. Men home from war, living normal lives, suddenly hacking up Scratch the dog with souvenir bayonets. And that was the ones who had been there a year, not thirty.

Renwick shudders. At the bar, there will be silence. No one will ask him anything. Except the lawyer for Annie's estate, in court: "You knew she was with this maniac and you left her to her fate?"

He runs back across the lawn, starts up the lodge steps, then stops and decides stealth is in order.

He moves toward the shadows at the side of the building, turns the corner and loses the moon. He finds abandoned toys with his feet, stumbles and falls, gets up and falls again.

Around another corner he finds a rectangle of light that extends from the open kitchen door. He looks in. Healthy young men and women—college students on summer vacation—are feeding dishes through a dishwasher, laughing and spraying each other with water. At some age, thinks Renwick, I stopped being one of them. I didn't even notice.

At one side of the kitchen, a railing disappears into a stairwell. Weena, thinks Renwick. Down there. She's stopped being one of them, too.

He turns and looks up the hill behind the lodge. The steaming roofless cabins of the pools, three of them, sit fifty yards up the slope.

Lights are on in all of them. Holes between the logs show as small bright points. People are in there, thinks Renwick. He doesn't want to think who they might be. But he makes his way up the hill anyway, until he's standing outside the door of one of them. He listens, but there is no sound. He moves the door. It creaks.

"What was that?" a woman's voice asks.

"It's nothing. The wind," says a man.

"I'm afraid he'll find out."

"I don't care. Let him find out. I hope he finds out."

"You think it's going to be that easy?" asks the woman. "You think he'll say 'Oh, go ahead, you love each other, it's okay?'"

Renwick opens the door and looks in. The waiter and the Madonna of the Helicopters stand naked in the water.

"This one's taken," says the waiter.

"I was looking...." says Renwick.

"She's not here," says the waiter.

Renwick closes the door, then opens it. "Have you seen...." he begins.

"Get out before I break you into pieces," says the waiter.

Renwick ducks back and slams the door and tiptoes to the next pool. He avoids the door, and goes instead to a corner and begins to climb, using the log-ends as steps. He jams his feet between them, digs his fingers into rotten wood, and pulls himself upward. Near the top he misses a step. He hangs for a while by his fingernails, his feet drumming against the logs.

"Weena?" says a loud voice. It's Cash. "Weena? Is that you?"

Renwick presses himself against the logs until his feet find holds. Then he works his way up the last few inches of wall and peers down into the pool.

Cash, naked and bulky, is swaying on the pool edge. He looks toward the door, sees it's closed, and begins walking toward Renwick's perch. Renwick ducks behind the logs.

"Weena?" says Cash. Renwick can hear short emphasymic breaths just inches away. "Women," says Cash. "Never there when you need them. When you don't need them, they're there and they bother you."

Silence. Renwick, his arms burning, pulls himself up and peers over the wall again, just as Cash falls back into the water and splashes a gallon or so of water over the wall and onto Renwick. Cash floats in the center of the pool, eyes closed, with a grin on his face.

Renwick hears falling rain. Cash, making like he's holding a tiny fire hose, is pissing in the pool.

Renwick lowers himself slowly down to the boardwalk.

"Weena," yells Cash.

Renwick walks to the third pool. Light and steam are streaming into the night from its open door. He goes to the doorway and stands in it.

In front of him is the pilot, sitting in the water, staring straight at Renwick. Beside him, her back to Renwick, is Annie. Their clothes hang behind them on the logs. Scars crisscross the pilot's skin.

As Renwick watches, Annie touches the man's chest, softly pushing her palm against the scar tissue. The pilot turns toward her. Then she puts her arm behind his back and draws him over on top of her.

Renwick turns and walks away, his eyes blinded by the after image of a single bulb reflected in the thousand ripples of the pool.

Halfway down to the lodge, he sees a group of people, all without clothes, running out the kitchen door. It's the band and fifteen or twenty young girls carrying beer. Groupies, thinks Renwick, wondering how long it would take him to learn to play the guitar.

They all run past him. Renwick hears the angry voice of the waiter, but it's drowned out by shouts and splashes. "Come on in," bellows Cash, in his pool. "Make yourselves at home."

People start into the pool occupied by Annie and the pilot, but stop in the doorway. They turn and run back toward Cash's braying laughter.

Renwick walks to the kitchen door and rests his head against the doorcase. He closes his eyes. There were other women he could have asked. Words for his tombstone.

He has a sudden sure knowledge that Cash has orchestrated everything. Cash ordered them placed at his table. He had introduced her to the pilot, for whom nothing was too good.

What Renwick sees, upon opening his eyes, is the stairway to the cellar. He walks through the kitchen door and over to the stair rail. It's dark down there. The stairs, steep and rotting, end at a closed door. Is Weena behind it? He doesn't think so. She was just a ruse to lure him away from Annie.

But. No. Wait. Cash was calling for Weena. He didn't know where she was. Renwick remembers Weena's kiss and the close press of her body.

She might be down there, he thinks. He looks down the stairs, then holds onto the rail and tiptoes down. He reaches the door, pushes it open far enough to admit his body, and enters a warm, misty darkness.

The light from the stairwell shows only a damp dirt floor and a few feet of concrete wall on either side of the door. He gropes for a light switch but finds nothing. It's hot. The springs, he thinks. The lodge is below them, and here in the cellar there is the slow seep of hot water. He hears the interwoven humming of a dozen electric motors. It's a too hot a place to put refrigeration equipment. It probably runs all the time.

"Close the door," someone says.

Renwick squints into darkness. The taste of sulfur stays on his tongue after every breath.

"Close the door and I'll turn on the light."

Renwick pushes the door shut.

"Dark in here, isn't it?"

"You said you'd turn on the light."

"Try to see your hand in front of your face. You can't do it."

Renwick tries to find the doorknob, but it's gone. "TURN ON THE LIGHT!"

"Okay, okay. Don't yell."

The light from a bare bulb, too bright for his eyes, shows him Weena, cowboy hat and all. She's stretched out on a large chest freezer in the middle of the room, resting on hip and elbow. With her free hand, she has reached up to grasp the string dangling from the light. He looks around. Mushrooms—huge, white, poisonous—growing together in incestuous families, are all over the floor, making it look like a slum for degenerate elves. Narrow boardwalks run above the floor, and the mushrooms under them are flat and distorted, their caps intertwined and pushing up through the planks.

"You've kept me waiting," says Weena.

"You all planned to take her away from me, didn't you?"

Weena smiles. "No. We never plan anything." She beckons him closer. He goes to her, stepping around mushrooms. She takes his hands in hers.

"It's a game, isn't it?" he asks. "An ugly game you play with guests."

"No game," she says, kissing his forehead. "Whatever happened is between you and your Annie."

"She's not my Annie."

"She found something. Women do sometimes find something they want." Weena pulls him up, with surprising strength, onto the enameled surface of the freezer.

"She's with the pilot," he says. "She's out in one of those pools with the pilot."

"You want a popsicle?" Weena asks him. "This freezer's full of them."

She takes his head in her hands and kisses him on the lips. She tastes like sweet popsicle syrup. Root beer. He notices millions of little dew balls of sweat on her face.

"Nobody took her away from you. She just went. Women leave men all the time."

Weena smiles. "No matter. Down here, it's just us." She gestures at the fungus-laden ceiling. "Don't worry. No one will come."

She presses his hands to her breasts.

"There are advantages in being abandoned," she says. "You can get seduced."

"Seduced?" he asks. I didn't ask for this, he thinks. It's not my fault.

She releases his hands and he puts his arms around her. He kisses the damp skin above her collarbone. She unbuckles his belt. He runs his lips up her neck and breathes in her ear. She unzips his fly and tugs at his pants. He leans back, levering his hips off the freezer. She pulls his pants and underwear down to his ankles.

"I should have taken off my shoes," he says.

"They won't get in the way," she says. She jumps off the freezer and lifts his legs up onto its surface, then pushes him down so he is on his back, stretched out on the metal.

"You'll have to forgive me," she says. "I'm shy." She turns off the light.

It is as though he's never needed eyes. The darkness, hot and wet, encloses him.

He puts his hands out to the edges of a controllable world. "Weena?" he asks. He can hear her taking her clothes off.

"Just lie back," she whispers. "This will be all for you."

"Turn on the light."

"Wait until we get to know each other better."

He feels her climb up and straddle him, feels the pressure of her broad thighs on either side of his, and feels the deft touch of her fingernails as they move down his ribs to his belly, move back up along the line of hair to his navel and chest, and trace the faint lines of muscles and veins in his neck.

He's becoming conscious of a new sensation, in this being-taken-care-of. To just lie back—it's a pleasure that makes him recollect myriad past affairs as frantic, forced unfulfilled searchings. He remembers Annie, being led through the intricate moves of dance, and is certain that she found delight not in the moving but in the being led.

Now, with Weena ministering over him in the velvet black, Renwick finds it in his heart to forgive Annie, to understand her willingness to do Cash's bidding, and even, in her turn, to lead the poor, wounded pilot to grace.

"Just lie back," says Weena, again. Her voice soothes wounds he cannot remember, scars he cannot reach. "Lie back," she says.

But—it's an old habit—he reaches up for her breasts and finds them, turgid and swaying, above his face. Her nipples push out between his thumbs and forefingers, and—just to see if he can do it—he pulls them against each other, rubs them back and forth until they stiffen, excited by their own friction.

Weena sighs, her voice hoarse and disembodied, from miles above him. He wants to lean forward, put his nose against her sternum and wrap her breasts around his ears, shake his head and feel them quiver like great sea creatures. He wants to drown and drift with them through submarine canyons. Death, he thinks, in happy recognition. It's pure inert pleasure.

Weena pushes his hands down to metal. "Don't want you to have to move at all."

He'll meet her in alleys and under bridges. He'll turn to her in the corners of galleries, discover her suddenly thrust against him in phone booths, find her waiting for him in the back seats of junked cars.

She shifts, and he loses her touch. She's separate for a delicious moment.

Then he feels the wafting of air against his throbbing skin, and finally her enveloping touch. She sighs, relaxes, and pushes down around him, holding the rest of herself away.

Gradually he loses track of where he is. Only faintly, as through a curtain, can he feel hands gripping the top of a freezer, or fingernails digging into the rubber seal that rims it. Only faintly can he feel toes curling in shoes. Only faintly can he hear Weena saying, "Oh. That feels GOOD!"

He arches upward pushing as hard and as far as he can, lodging himself in some far center.

He wants to grab her by her wide hips and bounce her madly, but he doesn't. Wait, he's telling himself. Let it—her—do it all. Stories he's heard but not believed—tales swapped across the bar, the accounts of travelers just back from the Far East, articles in the Reader's Digest, all hinting at the incredible, that woman can be man's salvation—are gaining credence.

"Good for you?" Weena asks, moving slowly.

An oscillating groan is his reply. Lines of force begin moving toward his crotch. The universe shrinks, compresses, centers on a point.

"God," he moans, having gained insight into Her nature.

Weena stops. Renwick, hanging on the edge of divine singularity, becomes slowly aware of the sound of refrigeration.

"Don't stop," he says. But she stops.

Then he hears, beside him, breathing. Feet shuffle on a dirt floor. Someone is standing behind his head.

"Weena?" he whispers. "Weena, there's somebody in here with us."

She is absolutely still. Someone really is there. Renwick hears a hoarse giggle, and then footsteps.

Renwick prepares to die. It has to be Cash. He's slipped into the cellar during their frenzy and has stood there, close, until he's made sure who it is desecrating his popsicle freezer. In a second a light will go on and Cash will shoot him between the eyes.

When light comes, it is only from the door to the stairs being opened. Renwick sees movement, but then the door shuts and he can see nothing. He hears feet on stairs. Whoever it is has left them for awhile. They've got to escape.

"Weena?" he says. She hasn't moved.

"Weena?" he says, louder. No answer. He reaches up, but he can't find her. She must be leaning away from him.

"Where the hell are you?" he asks. He's still lost inside her and

134

she isn't moving. She must be having some sort of fit. His hand catches the string of the light switch and he pulls it.

Weena is gone. Renwick looks down. A gigantic pale mushroom, twelve inches across, bobbing up and down with every beat of his heart, is impaled on the brave engine of his manhood.

For one beat, two beats, three beats, Renwick watches the mushroom. Then he screams and throws it against the wall. It leaves a wet starburst sliding slowly down the concrete. He pulls up his pants.

He'll find her. He'll drag her deep into a pool and hold her there until she quits bubbling. He'll search through the lodge for her, smashing doors and breathing gutteral consonants at cowering men and women in cowboy-print pajamas. Then, he'll—.

No. They'll laugh. Even now, behind the hum of machinery, creaks in floorboards, the squeak of logs against each other as they cool in the night, he hears giggles, whoops and snorts, and the slaps of hands on distant knees. He hides his face in his hands.

He'll leave. He'll get in the Porsche and coast backwards, down the lawn to the gate and beyond, and only then start the engine. No one will hear him go. As for Annie—he remembers Annie—she can find her own way back.

But when he walks toward the door he hears footfalls on the stairs.

It's Weena, he thinks, coming back down to hear him moaning endearments in the dark.

He switches the light off, and waits, ready to spring. The door opens.

Light from the stairwell shows a skeletal, trembling man, chrome-bright with scars, who goes to the wall beside the door and slides his palms over the concrete.

Renwick turns on the light. The pilot spins toward him in a defensive crouch, sees him, looks toward the open door, looks back and falls to his knees.

"Don't tell them I'm back here," he says.

Renwick goes to him. "What are you doing?"

"You're not another psychiatric officer, are you?"

"No. I'm a bartender."

"Thank God." The pilot gets to his feet. "They come down here and take me up there. Make me dance."

He turns and inspects Renwick. "I remember you. You were with the woman."

"Annie?" Annie.

"Was that her name?"

"You didn't get her name?" asks Renwick. "She was in the pool with you. She was—touching you!"

The pilot looks sad. "Sorry. I don't remember everything that happens."

"What'd you do with her?"

The pilot appears not to hear him. "They took my clothes again," he says. "They often take my clothes."

"You were with her in the pool. You both—you had your clothes off."

"The problem," says the pilot, "is that you grow to despise space. Down here, there are walls. It's warm. Out there, you're flying at seventy thousand feet. No air. It's freezing. You can't breathe."

"You took her away," says Renwick.

The pilot shakes his head. "I did something wrong, didn't I?" he asks. "I remember bits of things. That's all. You don't understand. Nothing can live out there. The people you talk to are ghosts. You can grin at them, wave, and follow them if you feel like it. But they don't show up on radar."

"What did you do with her?" Renwick asks, low and deadly, and he grabs the pilot and pushes him against the wall. The man's head snaps back, bounces forward. A twitch of agony rides muscles through the face.

"That's good," the pilot says. "The pain. They forget the pain here. Without the pain it's only half a world." A grin shows new teeth.

"What did you do with Annie? Please tell me."

"The woman?" The pilot smiles. "I didn't do anything with her. At least I don't think so. She was with me for a while this evening. Then she went away."

"Away?" Renwick asks.

Annie must be back at the cabin. Waiting for him. She'll be in bed. His side of the bed will be turned down.

"Hop in," she'll say with a smile.

"I can't," he'll say. "I have a fungus infection."

"Try to think," the pilot says, "of life in a cage for thirty years. The faces outside the bars are the same faces. Your hands are the same hands. The bars are the same bars. You know what happens?"

"You go mad," says Renwick.

"I know where I am." the pilot whispers. He pushes off the wall. Renwick backs away, leaving footprints in mushroom flesh.

"I know where I am," says the pilot, his voice rising. "I know it's the United States of America and I'm a released prisoner-of-war and I've got enough money from combat pay to buy myself a home and a new car. Fly for an airline. Go back to my wife and kids."

"That's a good idea," says Renwick, wanting to agree.

The pilot shakes his head. "You can't live with phantoms," he says. He turns to the wall and smacks it with his fist.

"This you can live with," says the pilot, staring down at four flaps of skin that are hanging off his knuckles. "Walls mean what they seem to mean."

"What are you doing here?" Renwick asks.

"I'm not doing—DOING—anything. I'm supposed to be with normal people doing normal things. They said I was not reintegrating well."

The pilot walks past Renwick to one of the freezers and opens it.

"You want an ice-cream sandwich?"

"No," says Renwick.

The pilot throws a frozen paper-wrapped brick of ice cream at Renwick. Renwick catches it and gazes at it, uncomprehending. It has a small world embossed on its wrapper, the ice-caps run wild, covering everything but a strip around the equator.

The pilot maneuvers into a gap between the wall and the freezer. There, rags have been piled into a bed. The pilot sits down on them.

"I used to be able to name thirty-nine flavors of ice cream," says the pilot. "Baskin-Robbins never heard of any of them."

"I'm going to go," says Renwick.

"For thirty years," says the pilot. "I was a U.S. Air Force major, serving my country, refusing to confess to war crimes, and building houses, stick by stick, in my mind. First I built a nice house in the suburbs. Then a vacation cabin by a lake in the mountains. Then a treehouse for my kids. Then—."

Renwick feels something run over his hand. His ice-cream sandwich has begun to melt out of its wrapper. He throws it down.

"I'm out of here," he says.

"Wait," says the pilot. "I lived for your dead country. At least hear me out."

Flashback. A line of cops and dogs, moving against a mob of students, and Renwick throwing books, bottles, bookends out his dorm window, but it's too far, nothing he can do can do any good—resonates with what the pilot says. Dead country. Country of death. Living carries the horror of watching cops and dogs move toward people like yourself. Renwick waits for the pilot to speak.

"One day I'm sitting there in the cage and building a gazebo in the back yard—of my mind, of course, right next to the swing set—when suddenly it comes to me."

Silence. "It?" says Renwick, finally.

"That day," says the pilot, "I realize it's not just gazebos and houses that are imaginary. It's being in the Air Force. My combat pay, adding up in an account. My wife and kids. Ski vacations. My '63 Impala SS I bought when I graduated from the Academy. My name, my rank, my serial number. None of these were real. Look."

The pilot stands up, his bony chest thrust out. The scars, thinks Renwick, seeing them plainly, in the light. Not all of them are random. The ones across his chest stand out from the dead skin, fluorescing a little, and spell: ONLY THIS IS REAL.

"The cage," says the pilot. "My captors, who I watched grow old. The rain and sun. The vines that grew up through my floor."

Renwick touches his own chest. A question.

"I did it," says the pilot. "With a nail." He points at the ceiling. "Up there, I push against the words. I can read them from the inside."

Renwick understands more of this than he wants to. In the last few months he's come home nights, drunk, and gone into the bathroom and stared at the mirror until his image has shifted, flattened, become tinted with streaks of neon purple, then lost big chunks of itself to the silver surface. He's always panicked before he's disappeared completely, and has run out and seen what's on the tube.

He walks to the door.

"You won't tell them I'm here?" asks the pilot.

"Not a word," says Renwick.

"Come down again," says the pilot. He sits back down on the rags, a placid smile on his face, his legs crossed, gazing out over mushrooms.

"You want me to turn off the light?" asks Renwick.

"Please," says the pilot.

Renwick goes to the light, turns it off, and runs through the door and up the stairs. The kitchen is deserted. A fluorescent light wavers above the sinks and the shroud of the dishwasher, showing cold stoves and racks of pots.

He looks for Weena, hoping to find her leaning into a refrigerator, rooting down among the Tupperware cultures, so he can push her in and slam the door. But she is gone.

The whirr of fans is the only sound. Renwick wonders about the power bill. Cash must have to equip whole armies to keep his ice cream cold.

He pushes open the door. Faint laughter comes from the pools. People are up there having a good time. He has an urge to join them, to run up, to strip off his clothes, to dive in and come up unfungused into the arms of people glad to see him.

But not if Annie's there. He's sure she is, probably in the arms of Cash, who's pinching the fat on her upper arms to see if she'll grace his Ferrari. Or she's standing on the edge of a pool, naked, her hair full of starlight. Everyone else is in the pool, kneeling on the bottom, worshipping her with a litany of bubbles.

He turns away from the hill and begins to stumble along the lodge walls to the front lawn. Feeling his way through the tiny dump trucks and GI Joe dolls that children—he wouldn't want to say whose—abandoned at the end of a make-believe day, he sees, one final time, scenes framed by the lit windows of far-distant cabins:

—Himself, counting tips at the dead end of a shift, walking home through three a.m. silence, turning on CNN.

—His apartment, its windows dust-frosted in peeling frames, his car, accumulating ever more dents, his friends, disappeared into careers, his town, Gomorrah, which, most days, he no longer recognizes under its burden of fresh turf.

—Women, dozens of them, beginning with his baby-sitter for whom he felt what he now recognizes as a nascent itch, and ending years later—he chooses this ending over one more painful—with Annie, on a rented bed, pulling on spike-heeled boots, about to betray.

And so at the lawn he stops and counts cabins until he locates his. Its windows are dark. He'll go in, pick up his bag and go. He crosses the lawn, walking under helicopter blades, and opens the door.

"Renwick?" asks a sleepy voice. Annie is in the bed.

"What are you doing here?"

"Renwick, I'm sorry."

She turns on a bedside light. In its glow, he sees her clothes on a chair beside the bed.

"I didn't mean to leave," she says.

He looks at her hair on the pillow.

"Maybe it was an accident," he says. "Maybe it's an accident that I'm going now."

She looks up at him. "How will I get back?"

"You'll find a way."

Then he's shouting, asking her how she could do this to him when the weekend meant so much to him, when he's asked her along even though he knew it wasn't a good idea to date co-workers, when he liked her, doesn't she understand? He doesn't like these people, the ones who own the lodge and if she'd had any idea how uncomfortable dinner was for him she would have stayed by his side and they could have left then, and none of this would have happened.

"I said I was sorry." Annie's going back toward sleep again, too tired to care he's trying to hurt her.

Renwick picks up his bag. "See you in Gomorrah."

But she makes one last attempt to wake, props herself up on an elbow and reaches toward him. The sheets on the bed, he notices, are satin. "Please don't go," she says.

"Get dressed," he says. "You can go with me."

"Come here," she says.

He puts down his bag, thinking does she know I can't help this? She grabs his hand, not appearing to notice it's sticky with ice cream. He sits down on the bed.

She puts her hands on either side of his, and puts her head against his thigh.

If she says she smells mushrooms, thinks Renwick, I'm out of here.

But Annie says nothing. They stay unmoving, both of them silent, until Annie begins to snore. Renwick reaches over with his free hand and strokes her damp hair.

Sometime in the night he sleeps and has this dream:

It is before dawn at the ranch. He is in a helicopter, holding Annie in his arms. They watch the pilot walk toward them, his combat boots leaving tracks in the damp grass. He sits in the seat beside them. There is a turbine whine and the slap of blades against air. Through plexiglass, Renwick can see Cash and Weena and the waiter and the Madonna of the Helicopters waving good-bye.

Airborne, Annie turns to Renwick and kisses him. He feels her lips soften against his, feels her body beneath her satin flight jacket. Over her shoulder, Renwick can see the pilot, with one hand on the stick and the other over his heart, pulling them up to the mountains, to the high clouds of the sunrise, to the sun. Renwick gazes down at the guest ranch, at the wind-blown tops of peaks, at the earth.

Renwick, suddenly afraid, suddenly brave, smiles at Annie, holds her close, and takes great deep breaths of the brightening air.

FLOWERING

IT'S ANNIE. SHE'S SITTING IN THE
mountain-top restaurant with Suzanne and LaVicka, catching the
afternoon sun through the western windows, nursing a beer—on
ski days she allows herself one beer—and listening to LaVicka talk
about her new nose. LaVicka's not quite happy with it yet. She's
got to keep the sun off it for another month or it will sunburn and
really, truly, fall completely off, so she's covered it with a thick
layer of zinc oxide and she won't take off her sunglasses for fear
some old lover—God knows there are enough of those—will
recognize her and laugh. All LaVicka would need is a moustache
and a trench coat, Annie thinks, and she'd be all dressed up for
Halloween.

Oh, stop being a bitch, Annie tells herself, but then LaVicka
gets up to go to the restroom and checks the mirror.

"What do you think?" asks Suzanne.

"Not that much wrong with the old one," says Annie.

"With the old one at least she didn't look like Julie Nixon,"
says Suzanne, but then corrects herself. "Julie Eisenhower, I
mean. She stopped being Julie Nixon even before her father
resigned. She got his nose, though."

Suzanne keeps track of who gets married. It's a compulsion of
hers. Then Suzanne says, "If she was going to change something,
she should have started with her name."

"Likes her name," says Annie.

Suzanne laughs. "Can you imagine," she says, "parents that
cruel?"

"Umm," says Annie, noncommital.

"What would you fix," asks Suzanne, "if somebody gave you
the money for an operation?"

Annie doesn't even like the sight of knives, and the thought of

145

surgery—she's not going to think about it. But Suzanne needs an answer in a language she can understand. "Facelift, probably," says Annie.

"I have a friend," says Suzanne, "who took her divorce settlement and went for black market implants. Took a trip to Mexico and walked into the surgeon's office and said, 'Give me the biggest set you got.' You should see her."

"Should?"

"It changed her life. Men won't leave her alone. They're big. And these days, most people think they're real. She's trying to get her insurance to pay to change them back. It's completely ruined her skiing."

"Facelift," repeats Annie. "And not for men. Or man."

"Easy for you to say," says Suzanne.

What's that supposed to mean? wonders Annie, except she knows. She's been going out with Hardesty for a couple of months now and he used to be Suzanne's lover. Suzanne wanted to marry him. Suzanne is still bitter, claims Hardesty can spot a co-dependent woman a mile away. Annie's put up with the implied insult because Suzanne's sometimes funny and most-of-the-time smart, but Annie does get tired of being treated like she doesn't know what's going on. She's been keeping a secret from Suzanne, for humanitarian reasons, she thinks, or because she's been waiting for a moment like this one to spring it on her.

"Something happened," she says. "Hardesty."

"He's found a new sport," Suzanne guesses. "Hang-gliding. Fixed-object parachute jumping. Russian roulette."

Annie shakes her head.

"Quit his job?"

Annie shakes her head again, and says, "Managing big accounts now. Moving up."

"Whatever that means."

Annie smiles. "Wants me to have his baby."

Suzanne goes icy. "Sure."

"It's true. Asked me Groundhog's Day."

"Must not have seen his shadow," says Suzanne. Then: "If

you would do that," she says, "it would be just about the stupidest thing I've ever heard."

"Didn't say I would."

"The man's a child."

Annie just smiles some more at her and says, "Wants a big church wedding."

"You do what you want with your life. You're an adult. But don't come crying to me when it turns rotten."

"Didn't say yes."

"But you didn't say no, did you? If you marry him," says Suzanne, "it'll be the same thing as telling him you love him."

Suzanne's advice to her, for six weeks, has been to never tell Hardesty he's loved. "If he thinks you love him, if he thinks he's got you, it'll be all over," is what she says. Annie's gone along with it. Even since Groundhog's Day, even with the gifts and the dinners and the I love you's that Hardesty's been pushing on her, all she has said has been "nice." It drives him crazy.

"Mess up your life if you feel like it," says Suzanne.

Annie realizes she's messed up Suzanne's day. But she can't stop. "Maybe I didn't understand him right," she says.

LaVicka comes out of the restroom, hair six inches taller, a fresh coat of zinc oxide on her nose.

"I hate this," she says. All people look at is my face."

"Annie," says Suzanne, "is going to marry Hardesty and have babies."

"Really?" breathes LaVicka. "That's wonderful."

"No it's not," says Suzanne. "It's sad. It's tragic. It's ugly."

LaVicka misunderstands. "Wouldn't you like a little baby all your own?" she asks Suzanne.

The ski patrolman who has been sitting at the next table and listening to their conversation looks at his watch and tells them he's got to clear the restaurant. Everybody else has gone home.

LaVicka leads them out the door. Annie hangs back.

"Not Julie Nixon," Annie says to Suzanne. "Bob Hope."

Annie puts her skis on. The sun is still shining on top of Mammon, even though the lifts have stopped and the runs are empty.

Winter's going. Annie loves this time of year, this time of day, on Mammon.

Hardesty's told her he'll pick her up at the Moloch Gulch Lodge, on the north side of the mountain. Suzanne and LaVicka have their cars in the Gommorah city lot to the south.

"Ski down with us," Suzanne says. "We'll drive you around. It won't hurt Hardesty to wait."

Annie agrees, but she shakes her head and points her ski pole north. "Steeper over here," she says. "Got to play Olympic racer." She points at herself. "Goddess material."

LaVicka waves goodbye. "I'm really happy for you," she says. "We'll have a shower."

"Idiot," says Suzanne, not looking at either of them.

Annie skates away from them, thinking she shouldn't have told Suzanne, wondering why it is she almost always says the exact things that push people away. It's a failure of the language. Makes intimate girl talk impossible. If she had one close friend, somebody incapable of being offended, she would try to tell her how she really feels about Hardesty. No, she thinks. I wouldn't want a friend that close.

Then for awhile she isn't thinking at all, because she's shooting down the cat-track to the top of the run called Hellfire, jumping bumps on the easy slope at the top, then making smooth quick turns down the steepening slope at the bottom. Hellfire connects with Mephistopheles, long and steep, which connects with Ishtar which connects with the lodge at the bottom. She hits Mephistopheles, turns down the fall line so she won't get at cross purposes with the moguls, and holds it for as long as she can until she's going TOO fast and has to bounce and chatter sideways for fifty yards before she can stop.

You're not getting older, Annie tells herself. You're getting faster.

She smiles, thinking of Hardesty and his sudden ambition for her to become a mother. She's thirty-seven, no kids, and she's got a job waitressing in a restaurant where the tips are good. She's got a car that's paid off and a season pass to the mountain. She's got a body that's recovering nicely from the life she lived after she got divorced and this coming summer she's going to do her first triathlon. If Hardesty thinks she's going to trade all that for wife-and motherhood, he's batshit crazy.

Then she's not smiling anymore, because the three years between herself and forty are looking more tragic by the minute. A thought comes unbidden: I almost didn't have to think about it.

Forty and you don't have to worry about a life with children in it. It's an arbitrary cut-off point, she knows, but she also knows the biological and financial arguments against having kids at that age and is confident they will prevail against any blind maternal hunger that she might wake up with some morning. Among other things, helping your kid with her homework is not something you want to do at fifty.

Her. Her homework. Oh, God, thinks Annie. Why me? Why couldn't Hardesty have asked Suzanne? Or LaVicka? If he'd asked LaVicka six weeks ago, she could have saved the money for her nose job.

Annie remembers coming out of her marriage mostly intact, a virgin on some level, all thoughts of home and family safely locked in an airtight vault along with her ability to love. Her ex-husband had given her a generous settlement and quit his advertising career and had disappeared with his lover to a little antique shop in a Sodom suburb.

She had come to Gomorrah. Where better to spend the rest of your life, if you've got a fat CD in the bank and a blank space on your heart where some dreams had been?

There's a mogul patch on the right side of Mephistopheles, up near the trees. Annie glides over to it and eases down through it, checking hard on the tops of bumps, jamming her skis into the troughs, getting air but not too much, hanging herself up, not out, so that she looks like she's doing the impossible, bump skiing in slow motion. She's smooth and she's perfect and she's not even breathing hard when she comes to a stop a hundred yards above the top of Ishtar.

Hardesty won't get out of Annie's mind, probably because Suzanne's just come a little too close to calling her stupid. Annie knows what she's doing, choosing Hardesty for a lover, or at least she did until Hardesty proposed. Talk about secrets. She should tell Suzanne one more.

Annie's watched, fascinated, as Hardesty's thrown himself into lethal sports, free climbing and kayaking and extreme skiing and a half-dozen others where the score is kept by body count. The danger and the motion seem to help Hardesty stop being Hardesty and start being what he's doing. He doesn't have to wonder why he's on the planet. A hard question for him, thinks Annie, remembering last weekend, on the way to telemark Beelzebub Summit, when Hardesty pointed up at the peak called Lot's Wife and told her he'd telemarked it nine times.

"That mountain," he told her, "is my monument."

It's the sort of narcissism—Suzanne, who's read whole books on it, calls it that—that starts by trivializing mountains and ends by trivializing one's own life and other things as well. Like women. Annie's long ago given up being anything in Hardesty's eyes but some appendage to his hollow presence labeled GIRLFRIEND. "That woman," Hardesty echoes in her head, "is—" Uh-oh. THE MOTHER OF MY CHILDREN? And entirely different kind of appendage, with impossible specifications.

It's too bad, because Annie has chosen Hardesty for the same quality that drives Suzanne into a fury: Hardesty doesn't see beyond the mirror of skied slopes and conquered mountains and seduced women he hangs between himself and the world. If you're on the other side of the mirror, he can't reach you. You've got a man who's there and isn't there at the same time. Being with Hardesty, knowing that he can't really touch her, has allowed Annie to glimpse, in her solitary interior, the slow growth of intricate, delicate floral crystals: a self.

There's a ski patrolman looking up at her from the very bottom of Mephistopheles and another is standing above her, just out of shouting range, looking down. They're impatient with her, because she's keeping them from sweeping the mountain clean. They think she's a cripple, a turkey, a duck—all names they give to novice skiers who get caught on Mammon and have to spend a couple of hours sideslipping down. You never notice them when the runs are crowded but after everybody goes home there they are, skiing sideways. In a little while the guy above will ski down and offer her a toboggan ride to the bottom. Annie knows all this because she's been out with three ski patrolmen over the last ten years. She used to hang out in the patrol shack and help on sweep, even after ugly rumors began going around about her being the patrol mascot.

So she'll move when she feels like it. The sun's gone down but it's still almost warm and it's quiet and she likes it here. She's paid for her ticket. Let them get paid to wait.

So Hardesty wants a baby. She should have seen the signs. His hairline has been heading north and she's caught him checking it in the mirror a couple of times. He's been complaining about his knees and back and he's not planning any more suicidal December ascents of The Devil's Bedstead. He's started a job with a brokerage, and this time, instead of looking forward to spring slack, when he could work it so he'd get laid off and be eligible for unemployment, he's putting in overtime and is up studying half the night. It's just a new lethal sport where the fatalities come not from missed footholds or trees fallen across rapids, but from mis-calculated futures contracts and coronaries. And this time the nec-essary paraphernalia isn't climbing skins or helmets or rock boots, it's a wife and kids.

For Hardesty, at least, it'll keep him from having to answer those tacky questions of identity and purpose for twenty years or so. Who am I? A stockbroker. Why am I doing it? For them. Who is them? "Them," says Hardesty, "is my FAMILY." Hardesty will be content to follow his own mind around in circles for years.

Annie, safe behind the one-way mirror that Hardesty squints into, realizes she could be safe there for a good while longer. More than that, she could have someone back there with her. She wouldn't be mine, thinks Annie, she would be all her own. I'd teach her to see that. Annie remembers her pre-Hardesty days in Gomorrah, her drunken nights of dancing and hot tubs and strangers, and realizes the direction she is going now is inward, toward solitude. She's grateful to Hardesty for helping her to define the journey, at least. At the rate she's going, someday soon she might be safe in there, secure and sufficient on the inside, ready for a real friend.

Annie shakes her head. As dreams go, Hardesty's isn't bad. But there are plenty of things Hardesty hasn't thought about. Her gynecologist, for one, along with the gram of flesh he takes each year for the pathologist's microscope. Every test she's taken lately has required a second opinion.

And there are her years carrying a Dalkon Shield, years on antique versions of The Pill, years full of questionable sex partners—years married to one—her Fallopians probably look like they've been used for knotting practice by Cub Scouts. Her HIV test came back negative, but that was before Hardesty went through the Change.

How is it possible that LaVicka can be worried about her nose? Doesn't she know that women—and men, too, if Annie can judge from Hardesty's aching back and popping knees and drought-stricken follicles—come apart from the inside out? She imagines, and envies, LaVicka's healthy interior, its volume only dented a little from the work done on her nose: everything sturdy and simple, everything working, everything wet and slick with blind and happy faith, warmed with hope. A perfect place for a baby to grow. Hardesty really should pick on LaVicka. Annie's going to have to tell him that before it's too late.

She relaxes and lets her skis slide and run straight downhill. She's in a tuck and going forty miles an hour when she passes the patrolman at the bottom of Mephistopheles, doing sixty or better when she chatters through the short section of rough bumps under the Ishtar lift. A couple of wide turns on Ishtar, she's thinking, and it's across the bridge and into the arms of Hardesty, who will carry her skis to his car. Some things she will miss, but probably not for long.

But when she's across the bridge, sliding to a stop in front of the lodge, Hardesty isn't there. One of the girls who works in the restaurant comes out and motions to her. "You'd better come inside," she says, and doesn't reply when Annie asks if anything is wrong. Annie steps out of her skis and walks quickly across the deck and through the door.

Flowers. Tables of them, tables of roses and chrysanthemums and lilies. And a computer-drawn banner on the wall above them that reads I LOVE YOU ANNIE. And bottles of champagne in buckets of ice. And Hardesty's superior and the rest of the people that work in his office, standing around in a semi-circle. And Hardesty in the middle of it all walking toward her, saying, "Annie, will you marry me?" and handing her a bouquet. Annie can't believe it. They're narcissus.

She looks at him, at the flowers in her hand, at Hardesty's grinning colleagues, at the tables, at the liquor and at the banner. She's never felt more alone. And she sees, quite suddenly, what life is, because the men standing around her, and the flowers, and the waitress and all of it are death.

Hardesty and the rest of them are waiting for her answer. She realizes, with some surprise, that it will be a lie. She's always tried to tell the truth, even if it meant being almost mute, but this time she's going to tell a lie that will give her enough time to walk away from this place and these people and not look back.

"Sure," she says. "What the hell?"

ABOUT THE AUTHOR

John Rember grew up along the Salmon River in Sawtooth Valley, Idaho. He has an M.F.A in fiction from the University of Montana, and is writer-in-residence at Albertson College, in Caldwell, Idaho. He is also the author of *Coyote in the Mountains and Other Stories*.